"You crazy kids think you can walk all the way to Alder Creek? Don't you know what that country's like out there?" He gave Jeff's wrist a jerk. "I'll bet you don't even have a compass."

"Let go," Jeff said, trying to ease backward. The old man's fingers remained clamped on his wrist. "What are you doing?"

"I'm trying to save your worthless hides." He yanked Jeff toward the counter. "You don't have a compass, do you?"

"No."

The old man snorted. "I figured. And you probably wouldn't know how to use it if you did. And I suppose the only shoes you got are those things you have on."

Jeff glanced down at his sneakers. "I'd better go now."

"You're idiots," Darby shouted. "You're gonna get yourselves killed."

P. J. PETERSEN has written several books for young adults, including *The Boll Weevil Express*, *Here's to the Sophomores*, *Nobody Else Can Walk It for You*, and *Would You Settle for Improbable?*, all available in Dell Laurel-Leaf editions. He lives in Redding, California.

Going for the Big One

P. J. PETERSEN

LAUREL-LEAF BOOKS bring together under a single imprint outstanding works of fiction and nonfiction particularly suitable for young adult readers, both in and out of the classroom. Charles F. Reasoner, Professor Emeritus of Children's Literature and Reading, New York University, is consultant to this series.

Published by
Dell Publishing Co., Inc.
1 Dag Hammarskjold Plaza
New York, New York 10017

Laurel-Leaf Library ® TM 766734, Dell Publishing Co., Inc.

ISBN: 0-440-93158-4

RL: 4.5

Reprinted by arrangement with Delacorte Press

Printed in the United States of America

October 1987

10 9 8 7 6 5 4 3 2 1

WFH

For the Hamiltons and the Jarboes—
the best of neighbors

*Going for
the Big One*

1

Jefferson County Bates couldn't figure out why he was scared. Things were rough at home right then, but he was used to problems. All his life he had been saddled with two big ones—his crazy name and his ridiculous size. From kindergarten on, wherever they moved, he had been the smallest person in his class. Knowing that he was going to be the class joke —the scrawny kid with the funny name—he beat the others to the punch by calling himself Superrunt or Itty-Bitty Bates.

Again and again he told his story: "There was a car wreck, and I was born in the ambulance on the way to the hospital. I only weighed about two pounds. I was in the Jefferson County Hospital for months, and I ran up a bill for thousands and thousands of dollars. When my dad saw the bill, he said I might as well be named for Jefferson County because that's who I really belonged to."

He didn't spoil the story by adding that his mother had died in the Jefferson County Hospital.

But right now Jeff was scared, and it didn't make any sense. The past month had been the old story again. First, his father had announced he was giving up long-distance hauling in favor of a steady job and nights at home. Then they had moved to Cooperville, where everything was going to be better. Lucky Bates had gone off to work singing. By the end of the week he was staring out the window and checking the want ads. Finally he had quit and headed the red Peterbilt for Alaska, hauling a load of vegetables.

Only Grace, who had married Lucky last Christmas, was surprised. "You promised," she kept saying as if she had really expected Lucky to stick by what he said.

Jeff knew better. Lucky always meant what he said —at the time he said it. But things could change in a hurry.

The only surprise for Jeff was the way his stomach kept turning over. Thirteen years old, he had been through too many moves, too many jobs, even too many stepmothers to start getting scared now.

But he couldn't shake the feeling. Part of it was spooky Grace. Ever since Lucky left, she had quit looking at them. And then today she had given them money and chased them off to the movies. His sister, Annie, was sixteen and didn't want to go to the kiddie matinee, but Grace had insisted, saying she needed a little time to herself.

Jeff was glad when the movies were finally over. He hadn't been paying attention anyway, and he wanted to talk. "I have a funny feeling in my stomach," he told Annie as they walked out into the bright July sun.

"It serves you right for eating all that licorice," Annie said. She was disgusted with him for buying a child's ticket to the movie.

Jeff couldn't see the problem. A cheap movie was one of the only benefits he got for being a runt. He had saved a dollar and used it for popcorn and licorice, which Annie wouldn't touch.

"It was those jerky movies," his brother, Dave, said. "They'd make anybody sick." As usual, Dave was walking two steps behind them, probably pretending not to know them. Anybody could tell they were related, though. All three of them had Lucky Bates's round face with straight black hair and dark eyes. Dave had on his motorcycle jacket, which he always wore in a new town.

"I'm not talking about being sick," Jeff said. "I just have the feeling that something's wrong."

"What's the big mystery?" Dave said. "Old Grace is about to cash it in."

Jeff looked back at him. "You think so?"

Dave shrugged. "She'll probably drag it out awhile, but I wouldn't worry about what to buy her for Christmas."

"It's Daddy's fault," Annie said. "He promised her he'd try it for three months anyway. And now she's stuck here with us while he's off to Alaska."

Dave snorted. "Anybody dumb enough to believe old Lucky's promises deserves what she gets."

"I knew we wouldn't be here long," Jeff said. "Dad always liked coming up here to fish and pan for gold, but he was always bored before the week was o

"Maybe old Lucky'll find us a place in Al
Dave said. "We can go up there and freeze
off with the Eskimos."

They turned the corner and headed down Holland Street. Jeff stretched out his arms. "Just look around. Alaska might not be so bad."

Of all the places they had lived, the house on Holland Street was one of the worst—a run-down shack wedged between other run-down shacks. All the front yards were filled with dry weeds and car bodies and old refrigerators.

"I can't believe it," Dave muttered. "We move clear up here to live in a slum."

Jeff cleared his throat. "I made up a poem in honor of this place," he announced.

> Holland Street
> Is hard to beat
> If you like weeds to your knees.
> If you saw paint,
> You'd prob'ly faint,
> But there's a bumper crop of fleas.

"That's terrible," Annie said.

"Don't be like that," Jeff told her. "I spent all morning making it up. I'm working on a second verse, but I need a word that rhymes with *garbage*."

Sitting on the front steps of their house was Mrs. Locke, who lived in a tiny cabin next door. A batch of kittens scampered around her huge ankles.

It was typical, Jeff decided, that the only person in ̱erville who had been friendly was a woman a̱̱d long conversations with her cats. He began ̱̱oem:

> ̱e craziest person on our block
> ̱ old lady named Mrs. Locke.

"Shut up," Annie said. "What do you s
doing on our steps?"

"She's probably lost," Dave said. "Most of t.
her dipstick doesn't touch oil."

When Mrs. Locke spotted them, she nudge
kittens aside and hoisted herself to her feet.
kids."

"Hello, Mrs. Locke," Annie said.

Dave moved up the steps past the old woman.
"Just a second," she said, breathing heavily. "Wait.
Don't go in there yet."

Hearing that, Jeff dashed up the steps and followed
Dave through the door. In the movies that line
meant there was a dead body inside.

"Wait!" Mrs. Locke shouted.

Scared and a little sick, Jeff moved ahead. Because
he was looking for a body, he had gone through the
living room and halfway across the kitchen before he
really noticed anything. Then it struck him: The
place was empty.

"She got everything," Dave yelled from the bedroom.

Mrs. Locke followed Annie up the steps. "Two
men in a truck loaded the stuff not half an hour after
you kids left. At first I thought it was burglars, but
then I saw your mama with them."

"She wasn't our mama," Annie said. "She was just
something Daddy brought home." She banged the
door closed.

On the counter by the sink was a twenty-dollar bill
and a note. Jeff read the note quickly, then shouted,
"Listen to this. Here's Grace's last shot: 'I got nothing
against you kids. But I got plenty against your father.
Take care of yourselves. Love, Grace.'"

'm surprised she left a note at all," Annie said.

Vhile Dave swore, Jeff crumpled the note and be-
n to laugh. "It's perfect. Only a fruitcake like
race could run off with your bed and then tell you
o take care of yourself."

"We ought to call the cops," Dave yelled. "She
robbed us. That TV wasn't hers. Old Lucky bought it
before she ever came along."

They plodded through the house. Their clothes
had been taken out of the dressers and tossed into
piles on the floor. Nothing else was left but a piece of
soap in the bathroom and two empty jam jars in the
kitchen. Even the light bulbs were gone.

"She took my lipstick," Annie said, leaning against
the kitchen sink. "And that blue blouse I bought last
week."

In the bedroom Dave was swearing and kicking
the wall.

"I'm glad I always hated her," Jeff said. "If somebody I liked had done this, I'd be really upset."

Annie almost smiled, then closed her eyes.

"I feel a poem coming on," Jeff shouted.

> Grace, Grace,
> I hate your face.
> When you left this place,
> All you left behind was empty space.

That time Annie did smile. "Not as bad as usual,"
she said.

"I'm surprised she didn't take the toilet paper,"
Dave yelled from the back of the house.

"The old girl wasn't all bad," Jeff said.

Annie opened a cupboard door, then slammed it
shut. "I can't see how anybody could be so hateful."

Jeff drifted into the garage. The only tools left behind were the broken lawn mower and a worn-out leaf rake. He glanced up at the rafters and let out a whoop.

Annie rushed through the door. "What's the matter?"

"She didn't get the camping gear," Jeff shouted.

Dave came and boosted Jeff high enough so that he could pull himself up to the rafters. Jeff handed down a dusty packframe. "You think she didn't see this stuff? Or did she just not bother with it?"

"Listen," Dave said, "if she stole the light bulbs, she'd steal anything, even these ratty old sleeping bags."

They spread out the gear on the empty kitchen floor: sleeping bags, two packframes, Lucky's gold pan, a canteen, the big mess kit, and the stove.

Annie pried open the mess kit. "We're all set now. We've got pans and forks and spoons."

Dave grabbed up a sleeping bag. "I got dibs on Lucky and Grace's room. If I have to sleep on the stupid floor, at least I'm gonna have a room to myself for a change."

"I'd better go to the store before it closes," Annie called after him.

"Get something good," Dave said. "How 'bout a pizza?"

"Forget it," Annie said. "This twenty bucks is all we've got. We'd better go real easy."

Jeff groaned. "Are we back to stale bread and soup again?"

Annie glared at him. "With all that licorice you ate, you shouldn't be hungry anyway."

After Annie left, a station wagon pulled into the driveway.

"Hey, Dave," Jeff called. "Somebody's here. A guy in a suit."

Dave pulled on his leather jacket. "I'll take care of him."

The man had his foot on the first step when Dave came out the door. Dave stopped at the top of the steps, crossed his arms, and asked, "You want something?"

Jeff watched the man's face twist into a glare. Dave had a way of sneering at people that always got that reaction.

"I'm Ray Carson. I own this place."

Dave looked at the house, then back at Carson. "You bragging or complaining?"

Carson stiffened, then looked at Jeff. "I hear you people are moving out."

"You hear wrong," Dave told him.

"Are your parents here?"

"Nope," Dave said. "I think they went to the opera."

Jeff leaned against the door and held his breath when he saw Carson's fists double. "Asking for it, aren't you?"

"I'm fifteen," Dave said. "You can get in big trouble hitting kids."

Carson glared, then turned away. "The rent's due Tuesday. You'd better have it, in cash, or be gone."

"We're not leaving," Dave told him. "We're getting to feel right at home. We know all the fleas and termites by their first names."

"Tuesday," Carson said and walked back to the station wagon.

"You're a real sweet talker," Jeff said.

Dave shrugged and pushed past him.

Grace had forgotten the light bulb on the back porch, so they ate their canned chicken noodle soup and day-old bread in a lighted kitchen. "We'll have to be stingy for a while," Annie said. "I'll write Daddy tonight, but there's no telling how soon he'll get it."

Before Lucky Bates took off on a long haul, he always picked a spot for a mail stop. This time it was a place called Tok Junction, Alaska.

"How long do you think it'll take?" Jeff asked. He knew that Annie had no more idea than he did, but he wanted to talk about it anyway.

"Four days or so," Annie said. "He should be able to wire us some money from there. A week at the outside."

Dave snorted and got up from the floor. "We'll see."

"We'll be all right," Annie said. "Maybe we can find some odd jobs or pick up aluminum cans."

"Rent's due Tuesday," Dave said.

Annie waved him away. "We can bluff the landlord a few days."

Jeff snickered. "No problem. He and Dave are old buddies."

"What's the big worry?" Annie said. "If he kicks us out, Mrs. Locke will put us up."

"Have you been inside her place?" Jeff asked.

"It's little and it stinks," Annie said. "So what? We can sleep out in the backyard."

"Grace, Grace, I hate your face," Jeff chanted.

* * *

That night each of them took a sleeping bag into a separate room. Annie moved the light bulb from the kitchen to the hallway outside the bathroom.

"Just leave it on," Dave said. "We ain't paying the electric bill anyway."

Jeff lay on his back in the empty room, his legs rigid, his stomach tight. He kept telling himself that it didn't make sense to be scared now. The bad thing had already happened. The Bates kids were going through a tough time, but they'd been evicted before. And they'd had stepmothers leave (although never the way Grace did it). Dave always moaned, and Annie always saw the good side, and somehow the three of them came through all right. Why should things be different now?

But things *were* different. The family was falling apart. Until they'd moved, Annie'd had a job. And Dave might leave anytime. Before, they had stuck together because they needed each other. But Annie and Dave could make it on their own now. And he was going to end up alone.

For the first time in years, he let himself think about Visalia. He had been nine then, and he hadn't even understood the process—the court hearings, the foster home, his father's visits on Sunday afternoons. Annie and Dave had been placed in a different home, and he hadn't seen them for months. And Jeff hadn't belonged to anything or anyone. He had been completely alone.

There it was. That was the thing that kept knotting his stomach. He could feel the family slipping away. At any moment Dave and Annie could be gone, and he would be left alone.

He quit shifting around on the floor and listened. Somebody was pulling into the driveway. It was much too quiet to be his father's Peterbilt rig. A minute later someone climbed the steps and pounded on the door.

Jeff pulled on his jeans and padded across the floor. Seeing car headlights through the window, he wondered if Grace had changed her mind and come back. Or maybe the landlord had decided to push in Dave's face after all.

Jeff pulled the door open a few inches and found himself looking straight at a badge. He stepped back and took in the man wearing it, a slim figure in khaki with his cap pushed back on his head.

"Is your mother or father home?" the man asked.

"I'm not sure." Jeff had learned long ago to keep his mouth closed around strangers, especially strangers in uniforms. "Is something wrong?"

"Yes, but I'd better talk to your parents about it."

Jeff banged the door shut and hurried across the house. Dave's sleeping bag was empty. Jeff glanced around, then went into the next room and shook Annie awake. While she pulled on a bathrobe and patted down her hair, she made him repeat every word the man had said.

Annie opened the door and smiled at the officer. "Yes?"

"Hello there. I'd like to speak to your parents."

"I'm sorry. They aren't here right now."

"Do you know when they'll be back?"

Annie yawned before she said, "I don't know for sure. Is there some kind of problem?"

"David Bates lives here?"

"Yes. He's my brother."

"We have him down at the substation right now. He's under arrest."

Jeff felt his knees buckle. He reached for the wall to steady himself.

"Under arrest?" Annie said. "What's he done? There must be some mistake."

"I don't think there's any mistake. I spotted him walking down the alley back there carrying a television that didn't belong to him."

"I see," Annie said.

"So we have a problem. We don't have any facilities here for juveniles. If your parents will be home pretty soon, we can keep him at the station and release him to them. Otherwise, we'll have to take him over to the juvenile hall in Martinsburg."

Annie looked over at Jeff and then at the officer. "A television? What on earth was he doing with a television?"

"You'll have to ask him."

"I just don't understand this at all," Annie said. "It's really strange. Listen, my parents may not be back till late. Could my grandmother come? Would that be all right?"

"Is she here?"

"She'll be back any minute," Annie said. "We'll come over to the station just as soon as she gets here."

The officer gave her the address, then went back to his patrol car.

"Dingaling's done it again," Jeff muttered.

Annie closed the door. "Get your shoes on, and let's go."

"You figure you can pass off Mrs. Locke as our grandmother?"

Annie headed for her room. "You have any better suggestions?"

They hammered on Mrs. Locke's door for several minutes before the old woman shouted, "Just a minute." She came to the door with a yellow blanket wrapped around herself, her white hair streaming across her face. "What's the trouble, darling?"

Annie explained the situation several times before Mrs. Locke began to nod. The old woman hitched up the blanket and sighed. "I don't think I can walk that far."

"We'll take it slow and easy," Annie said, following Mrs. Locke inside.

Jeff stood in the driveway, ignoring the cats that rubbed against his leg. It was just Dave's speed to steal a television, he decided. Dave could do without a bed or a chair, but he couldn't do without his Popeye cartoons.

And it was just Dave's speed to get caught. He was rotten at everything else—school, sports, everything. He was bound to be a rotten burglar too.

"Nice and slow," Annie said, opening the cabin door.

"You won't have no choice," Mrs. Locke said.

Jeff hadn't paid much attention when the old woman had said she couldn't walk that far. He was used to excuses. After a block, though, he knew that Mrs. Locke had been serious. Her breath came in long wheezes, and she kept stopping and leaning against lampposts or cars.

After the third block she had to rest. There was nowhere else to sit, so Jeff and Annie lowered her to the curb, where she sat with her feet in the gutter. She rested her head on her knees. When they tried to get her up after five minutes, she seemed to be asleep.

She walked between them, her huge arms draped over their shoulders. Jeff staggered along under the weight. When the old woman tripped, he thought all three of them were going down.

Mrs. Locke's breaths turned into moans. "Just a little bit more," Annie kept saying. "Just a little bit more."

Mrs. Locke stopped moving. "Res-rest."

"We'd better keep going," Annie said. But Mrs. Locke sank down. Unable to stop her, Jeff and Annie eased her to the sidewalk, where she lay curled in a ball.

When they got the old woman to her feet again, her head sagged forward, bobbing with each step. "Just a little bit more," Annie said between clenched teeth. "We're doing fine."

At the station Annie rang the bell. A deputy opened the door for them. He took one look at Mrs. Locke and helped Jeff and Annie ease her into the closest chair.

"Water," Mrs. Locke whispered.

The deputy dashed to a water cooler, filled a paper cup, and dashed back. While Mrs. Locke sipped the water, he took her other hand and began feeling for her pulse.

"We're here for David Bates," Annie told the deputy, who was looking at his watch as he held Mrs. Locke's wrist.

"Ma'am," he said, "do you have chest pains?"

Mrs. Locke had spilled most of the water down her front. She looked at him and smiled. "Honey, I have pains everywhere." She dropped her chin to her chest and closed her eyes.

"She just needs to rest a minute," Annie said. "She's been sick, and we had to walk all the way over here."

The deputy brought over a report on an official form. He seemed about to speak to Mrs. Locke, then turned to Annie. "Is she all right?"

"I think she's dying," Annie said. "The only thing that would have gotten her over here was keeping her grandson out of jail."

The deputy nodded. "All right. Your brother is being formally charged with being in possession of stolen property. He committed a burglary, and everybody knows it. But he's a juvenile, so there's no use pressing the point. He's to be at the county office building next door on Monday morning at nine o'clock. Your parents are supposed to come with him. He'll meet with a Mr. Edwards. The room number is on the sheet."

"This Mr. Edwards, is he a judge?" Annie asked.

"Caseworker. The hearing will come later, unless something gets worked out. But your brother had better be there at nine sharp."

"He will."

"He hasn't exactly made a lot of friends here. When Scotty spotted him with the TV, he didn't run. But he dropped the set and busted it all to pieces. And then when he came here, he did nothing but give us smart answers. Wasn't even going to tell us his name." He leaned over and spoke to Mrs. Locke. "Your grandson needs to work on his attitude."

Mrs. Locke looked up at him as if he were speaking a foreign language.

"Ma'am, would you like us to take you to the hospital? Just for a quick check-over? You're looking awful pale."

"Just tired," Mrs. Locke said, her head dropping again.

After bringing Dave from the back, the deputy radioed the patrol car. Scotty, the slim officer who had come to the house, gave them a ride home. The four of them squeezed into the back seat, separated from the front by a steel grate. When Scotty shut the door behind them, Jeff realized that there were no handles on the inside.

"I want you to know something," Scotty said over his shoulder. "They'll make you pay restitution. So I figure that little stunt of dropping the TV on the ground is going to cost you four or five hundred bucks. I hope it was worth it."

"That's—" Dave began, but Annie clapped her hand over his mouth. Dave shrugged and slouched back against the door.

Once the patrol car was gone, Annie and Jeff helped Mrs. Locke to her cabin. When they came back to the house, Dave was already in his sleeping bag.

"All right, Dave," Annie shouted, "I want to hear about it."

Dave turned toward the wall. "Leave me alone."

"You really did it this time. I can't believe it. You went out and stole a stupid TV."

"Lousy luck," Dave said. "The guy works nights and doesn't even lock his back door. If that dumb cop hadn't come by right then, nobody would have known."

"I'm glad you got caught." Annie kicked the middle of the sleeping bag.

"Cut it out!" Dave yelled.

"I don't care what they do to you," she said. "It's better than having this family turn into stealing, lying trash."

"Why didn't you just leave me there?" Dave shouted. "I'd rather sit in jail than listen to you."

"Oh, what difference does it make?" Annie walked out of the room.

"You did a great job tonight, Annie," Jeff said.

Annie reached out and squeezed his shoulder. "I guess we'd better get some sleep. Who knows what's going to happen tomorrow?"

"Well," Jeff said, "I know one thing. Dingaling in there won't be watching the Popeye cartoons."

When Jeff wandered into the kitchen the next morning, Annie had camping gear spread all over the floor. "What are you doing?" he asked.

"Checking to see what we need."

"Right now I need about three eggs and a pile of pancakes."

Annie looked up at him and snapped, "I don't need any of that. Things are a little rough around here, and I don't want to hear one word about what we don't have."

Jeff threw his hands in the air. "I surrender." He lowered his voice and said, "I was just joking, Annie."

Annie's glare softened. "And I was yelling like an old battleax. Sorry."

"That's okay. As soon as I get wide awake enough to think about Grace, I'll probably be yelling too."

"Go wake up Dave," Annie said. "I'm so mad at him right now, I don't want to go near him."

Jeff went straight to the bathroom, cupped his hands under the faucet, and carried the water into Dave's room. "Wake up, Dave." He trickled water onto Dave's neck.

Dave jerked sideways and burrowed into the bag. "What's the matter with you? What're you doing?"

"I thought maybe you were dead. I was just checking."

"You're gonna be dead if you ever do that again."

Jeff headed back to the kitchen. "As long as you're awake, you might as well get up for breakfast."

Annie was using a fork to toast bread over the burner of the camp stove. She handed Jeff two pieces and reached for more bread. "If you ask for butter or jam, you might get those stuffed down your throat."

"I like dry toast," Jeff said.

"Well, I hate it," she shouted. "It's nasty, and I can hardly gag it down, but it's all we've got."

Jeff carried his toast outside and sat on the front steps. The toast was a little chewy, but he finished both pieces quickly and went back inside. Annie shoved another piece at him. "Here. Take it. I can't stand to eat it."

Jeff took several bites before saying, "If you insist." Both Annie and Dave kept their eyes on the floor.

"Ladies and gentlemen, it's poetry time," Jeff announced.

> Grace, Grace,
> I hate your face.
> I hate you most
> When I eat dry toast.

    I wouldn't be as mad as I am
    If you'd have left us a little jam.

"Shut up, Jeff," Annie said.

Jeff held up his hands. "Thank you for not applauding. It embarrasses me."

Annie sat down on a rolled-up sleeping bag and glared at Dave. "We have to get out of here. We were lucky last night. Mrs. Locke scared them so bad they didn't ask many questions. But that caseworker's something else."

"So let 'em take me," Dave said. "I don't care. Jail can't be any worse than here. I'll bet they give you something besides bread for breakfast."

"After you spent a little time in jail," Annie said, "you'd be talking out of the other side of your mouth."

"I can take it," Dave said.

"Just shut up when you don't have anything to say. That social worker would want to know all about your family. And then there'd be somebody around here asking questions. And we'd all be in for it."

"Like Visalia," Jeff said.

Annie nodded. "Like Visalia."

"This is different," Dave said. "We're older now."

"Wise up!" Annie shouted. "We're still minors. You think they'd leave us here by ourselves in an empty house where the rent's overdue? I'm not worried about you. You deserve whatever you get. But Jeff and I aren't about to go to a foster home. You and your dumb TV."

Dave turned to face her. "Lay off that stuff. I mean it."

"All right." Annie's voice was softer. "We've got to

get out of here. You know that. And I've figured out a place to go."

"I vote for it," Jeff said. "I don't care where it is."

Annie smiled at him, then looked back at Dave. "You know that place we camped two summers ago while Daddy was panning for gold? White Bar?"

Dave nodded. "Yeah, I remember."

"That's the place. It's only about thirty miles from here. I've already written a letter to Daddy. We'll mail it on our way out. He can write us or wire us at the White Bar post office."

"White Bar?" Dave said. "Is that the best you can do?"

"It won't be so bad," Annie told him. "We can swim and fish and sleep under the stars. Beats sitting here in an empty house, even if that was possible. Remember those big trout we caught?"

Jeff began to sing:

> White Bar, White Bar, here we come,
> Annie, Jeff, and Brother Dumb.

"Shut up, Jeff," Annie said.

"How do we get there?" Dave asked.

Annie groaned. "Now how do you think? You figure we ought to take a taxi? Or maybe you think your pals at the sheriff's office will give us a ride."

"It's a long ways," Dave said.

Annie looked at him and shook her head. "And what else do you have to do today?"

II

Annie remembered the road from Cooperville to White Bar as a scenic highway running beside the Larkin River. Walking that road, she wondered how she could have forgotten the long steep grades. Heat waves rose from the pavement as they trudged up hill after hill, and Annie soon scrapped her plan of making thirty miles before dark.

Their two packframes were bulky and far too heavy, containing everything Annie could jam into them. The rest of their things had been left with Mrs. Locke. "I hate to think what that stuff's going to smell like when we get back," Jeff said.

Jeff insisted on taking his turns carrying a pack, although it hung down almost to his knees. When Annie tried to cut his turn short, he had a poem ready:

> I may be small, but that's all right.
> You could say the same about dynamite.

Annie's feet burned, and her shoulders ached, but she kept smiling. "You don't realize how pretty this country is until you walk through it."

"You've been out in the sun too long," Dave muttered.

Annie was used to pretending things were better than they were. With the bad luck that seemed to follow the family, she had had plenty of practice. By the time she was ten, she had quit believing her father's promises that things would be different in the new town or with the new woman. But for Jeff's sake, she kept smiling just the same.

Annie knew how important hope was. As long as Jeff believed he could whip the world, he just might do it. He did well in school, even with all the moving they did. And when things got rough, he came out with another of his silly poems.

With all the trouble they'd had, Jeff still had fire in his eyes. And he wasn't going to lose it—not if she could help it.

In the evening they moved away from the highway and spread their sleeping bags on a sandbar beside the river. Annie managed to put together supper without taking apart their whole packs.

"I'd rather be in jail," Dave said, sticking his sore feet into the icy water.

"I don't know about that," Jeff said. "The work's harder here, but the scenery's better."

"What scenery?" Dave grumbled. "All I've seen all day was blacktop."

"The worst part's behind us," Annie said.

* * *

Annie woke the others soon after daylight. The nine o'clock appointment worried her. After nine, hunting season was open, and Dave was a fugitive.

But nine o'clock passed, and they were still struggling up the same kind of hills. Annie began to watch the traffic, expecting a sheriff's car at any time. She carried her pack as long as possible, knowing that when Jeff took it, they would slow down.

It was late afternoon when they reached the White Bar Store, which sat in the middle of a scattering of trailers and tourist cabins. To celebrate, they bought cold root beer. Annie gritted her teeth at the price.

The White Bar post office was a booth next to the cash register. The old man who ran the place, Darby, sat perched on a stool with wheels, which allowed him to scoot from the register to the post office window without getting to his feet. Annie had to hold herself back from going up to the window and asking for mail. It seemed a long time since she had mailed the letter to her father.

Jeff was studying the topographic map on the wall, trying to locate the creeks where their father had panned for gold two years ago. Annie leaned against the wall and drank her root beer. She was too tired to care about maps just then.

Dave eased up next to her. "Buy some bread," he whispered. "I've got deviled ham and cheese and peanut butter."

Annie glanced down at the bulges in his shirt. "You put that stuff back."

"Don't be dumb."

Annie glared at him. "I mean it. Put it back—all of it."

"I can't do that. The old guy'll see me."

"If you can swipe it, you can put it back."

"I'll wait for you outside," Dave said. He took two or three steps before turning back. "Now you've done it. He's watching me."

Annie glanced at Darby out of the corner of her eye. "Put it all back."

"You're so dumb." Dave headed down the aisle.

Annie followed along behind him, picking up the items she wanted while he pulled things out of his shirt and put them back on the shelves.

After Darby rang up their purchases, he handed Annie the paper bag and winked at her. "You're a good girl."

The White Bar campground, which they remembered as being just down the road, turned out to be more than a mile away. To save the two-dollar camping fee, they headed into the manzanita and located an open space a hundred yards beyond the last campsite. Nobody paid any attention when they used the camp showers or came for a pan of water, but Annie still felt like a burglar.

The next morning the three of them cut willow branches and headed for the stream that ran past the campground. "I'm going to throw back anything over a foot long," Jeff said. "If it won't fit in the frying pan, forget it."

After two days they were discouraged and disgusted. They had followed two different streams for several miles. They had climbed over rocks and fought through the brush. And they hadn't caught a single fish. Their three-dollar jar of salmon eggs was nearly empty, and they had nothing to show for it.

"I still don't think we found the place where we caught those big ones," Dave said Wednesday night.

Nobody answered him. The argument had been running since noon.

"I'm telling you," Dave went on, "that wasn't the place today. It looked a little bit like it, but it wasn't the place."

"Who knows?" Annie said.

"I do," Dave said. "That wasn't the place." He turned toward Jeff. "I don't care what you say."

"Tomorrow morning we'll go to the White Bar Store, and I'll show you on the map," Jeff said. "And you probably still won't believe it."

"I don't believe it," Dave said when Jeff pointed out the spot on the map.

"I knew it was a waste of time," Jeff said. "No use confusing you with the facts."

Annie turned away from the map. "Mr. Darby," she called, "has anybody been catching any fish around here?"

"Things are pretty slow." Darby slid off his stool and ambled toward them. "They've been catching a few up on Twin Lakes. Mostly on Upper Twin." He stepped between Dave and Jeff and tapped the map with a knuckle. As he stepped back, he patted Dave's stomach. "Keepin' that shirt empty today, are you?"

"He was just joking the other day," Annie said. "He wasn't really going to take anything."

Darby looked at Dave, then back at the map. "If you're really after some fish, you might go on up past Twin Lakes to Hooker Lake here." His finger covered up a blue speck on the map. "There's not much of a trail, but the fishing is usually all right this time of year."

"Could we go in and out in a day?" Annie asked him.

Darby laughed. "Not unless you're pretty tough. It's about twelve miles one way."

"We're not that tough," Jeff said.

Darby smiled down at him. "If you want something a little easier, the breadman tells me there's pretty good fishing up by Alder Creek."

"Which creek is that?" Annie asked.

"It's a town, not a creek."

Jeff studied the map. "I don't see it."

"It's not on there," Darby said. "It's too far north." He reached up and tapped on the wall about a foot above the map. "It'd be about here, I reckon."

"How far is it?" Annie asked.

Darby smiled and shook his head. "Depends how you look at it. As the crow flies, it's about thirty miles. But to get there, you have to take the highway all the way to Brown's Crossing, then circle north. It's about a three-hour drive."

Annie studied the map for a minute, running her finger slowly up the wall. "What if we walked?"

"You'd still be better off going by the road," Darby said. "There's no trail on most of that."

"Forget it," she said.

"And there's crazies besides," Darby went on.

Annie was already looking at Hooker Lake again. "Crazies?"

"Lots of 'em. They're out there diggin' for gold or plantin' marijuana or chasin' Bigfoot. You don't want to mess with any of 'em." He walked back to the counter. "Not like the old days."

"Hooker Lake looks good," Annie said to the others. "We could go in there tomorrow, stay a day or two, then come back out. It'd be a good way to kill some time."

"Too far to walk for some dumb fish," Dave said.

Annie studied the map carefully before she headed down the aisle. She wouldn't argue with Dave just then. They wouldn't leave until the next morning anyway.

"White Bar," Dave said as they walked away from the store. "What kind of moron would stay around here if he didn't have to?"

"Daddy was thinking about living here and driving into Cooperville to work," Annie said.

Dave nodded. "That figures."

While Jeff and Annie marched single file along the narrow shoulder, Dave walked in the road itself. Oncoming cars had to cross the white line to avoid him.

"Will you move back?" Annie said after a driver shouted and laid on the horn. "Somebody's going to run over you."

"I'll sue 'em for everything they own." He held his ground while a pickup came toward them. The driver tapped his horn twice, but Dave didn't move.

Behind the pickup was a white car that none of them noticed until the pickup passed. Annie first saw the red and blue lights on top of the car, then recognized Scotty, the deputy who had taken them home. He shouted something as he passed.

The white car veered onto the shoulder and made a tight U-turn, its tires squealing. Dave dashed into an open meadow. The white car skidded to a stop across from Annie and Jeff. Scotty threw open the door and leaped out. "Hold it! Sheriff!"

Dave kept running.

Scotty grinned as he started forward with the easy lope of a distance runner.

"Dave's had it," Jeff said.

Annie watched Scotty closing the gap. Dave didn't have a chance unless— "Get back to camp," she yelled at Jeff. "Run!"

As soon as Jeff started up the road, she dashed to the sheriff's car. The front door stood open, the motor running and the radio squawking. Annie slid in behind the wheel. She watched through the windshield as Scotty gained on Dave. Then she pushed on the horn. The noise sent a shiver through her body, but Scotty didn't even look back.

Still holding down the horn, Annie glanced up for the switch that would turn on the siren. She was surprised to find it right where it had always been on TV shows.

When the wah-wah-wah of the siren began, Scotty looked back and shouted something, but he didn't break stride. He was only thirty feet behind Dave.

Annie moved the gearshift to Drive and stepped lightly on the gas pedal. She didn't even bother to shut the door as the car crept forward. She pounded on the horn. "Hey," she yelled, "I've got your car."

Scotty looked back, veered sideways, and sprinted toward the road. He yanked his pistol from its holster.

Annie watched him running toward her, shouting something and waving his gun in the air. She had waited too long. She couldn't run now. Scotty would have her in a minute.

She gripped the steering wheel with both hands and stomped on the gas pedal. The car leaped forward, the door banging shut beside her. Scotty dropped to one knee and leveled the pistol. Annie ducked down, shoving the gas pedal to the floor.

When she passed the entrance to the campground, she took her foot off the gas. The car slowed. She reached up and flipped off the siren.

She had just stolen a car—a sheriff's car. She, who had never been in trouble with anybody, had just stolen a police car. Her hands began to tremble, and tears ran down her cheeks. She reached for the brake and stopped the car in the middle of the road.

An old station wagon rattled past her. The driver stared at Annie.

She had to do something. Why not turn around and drive back to Scotty? Anything else would just make matters worse.

But what about Jeff? Where would he go? A foster home.

No! After Visalia, when the family had gotten back together again, Jeff kept waking up in the night, screaming. She wasn't going to put him through that again.

Annie drove forward slowly, looking for a wide spot. When she found one, she pulled the car off the road and left it. She was out the door before she thought of fingerprints. She leaned back into the car and used the tail of her shirt to wipe off the steering wheel and the door handle. As she dashed away she realized how silly it was to worry about prints. Scotty had recognized Dave; he wouldn't need fingerprints to know who she was.

At the edge of the campground she moved into the manzanita and crept to their spot. Jeff was already rolling up sleeping bags. "Annie," he said, "I'm glad to see you."

"Not half as glad as I am." She rushed toward him, stopped for a second as she came close, then reached out and hugged him. "How'd you get back here so fast?"

"I almost kept up with the car," he said. "Where'd you leave it?"

"Up the road. Did you see Dave?"

"Not after you took off." He tied the sleeping bag closed and grabbed another.

"Do you think he got caught?"

"No way. The deputy ran after you. Did you hear him shoot?"

Annie felt sick again. "Did he really shoot at me?"

"I think it was just a warning shot," Jeff said.

They stuffed all their gear into the packs, tied on the sleeping bags, and carried the packs into a thick clump of manzanita.

"Now what?" Jeff asked.

Annie lay down beside the packs. "We'll wait for Dave."

"You think he'll come back here?"

"Where else could he go?" Annie tried to think what to do next. They couldn't stay where they were, but Scotty would have the whole sheriff's department watching the road.

"You should have let him get caught," Jeff said. "He wasn't worth it."

Annie reached over and smacked Jeff's face with her open hand. "Don't you ever talk like that. Ever. He's your brother."

Jeff stared at her. "I'm sorry, Annie." He looked so pitiful that she reached out and squeezed his arm.

"And I'm sorry I slapped you. But I meant what I said."

Jeff rubbed his cheek. "You know what? That's the first time you slapped me since we were little kids."

Annie gave him a shove. "Watch out. It may not be the last."

"We'd better head for the back country," Jeff said. "Otherwise, we'll get picked up sooner or later."

Annie nodded. An idea was beginning to take shape. She wished that she had studied the map more closely. "Keep an eye out for Dave. I've got to write some letters."

III

Lies, Dave thought. *Lies everywhere. Nothing but lies. Just when you think you've discovered every rotten lie that has been laid on you, you turn around and stumble on another one.* For years he had heard about adrenaline, how people could do incredible things if they were scared enough: leap eight-foot fences, lift up cars, outrun horses.

With that deputy after him, Dave had been running for all he was worth, scared as he'd ever been. And what happened? The deputy would have nailed him in another hundred yards. Dave's sides had started aching so badly that he was ready to stop and give up when the siren went off. Then the deputy, probably worried about how dumb he would look having some girl swipe his car, had gone running back toward the road, shooting his stupid pistol. Dave didn't wait around to find out what he was shooting at.

Adrenaline! Dave snorted. That was another one to put alongside Santa Claus and Sunday School.

And families, he added as he thought about Annie. Just because you had the same parents, there was supposed to be something between you. More lies. Oh, you could train people that way maybe. Tell a kid too little to know any better that he's supposed to love his brother and sister, and he'll believe it. For a while anyway. But it was more of the same old bull. People were just like other animals. He'd watched litters of puppies push one another away from their mother's milk—each puppy looking out for itself, taking care of number one. That's just the way people were, except they wouldn't admit it.

Dave had moved beyond that kind of pretending. He knew his family for what it was. His father was a good-timing bum, who liked to play Daddy once in a while because it made him feel important. The rest of the time he was out on the road somewhere and couldn't care less.

And Jeff? What did he care about Jeff and his stupid poems and jokes? Little cute Jeff who always ended up top dog in the litter—the kind of kid teachers and old ladies were crazy about. What was Jeff to him?

And what was Annie to him? She had to be the dumbest sixteen-year-old girl on the face of the earth. She probably still believed in Santa Claus. You could show her what the crummy world was like, and she'd just smile and go on believing in fairy tales. Last winter, when he brought home a bag of oranges he'd swiped out of a parked car, she wouldn't eat any because they were stolen. What did she think was going to happen—her stomach was going to get contaminated? And then she let Jeff eat the oranges, but she made Dave promise not to tell him they were stolen. Figure that one out!

But today, when the deputy was about to run him down, Annie had climbed into the patrol car, whipped on the siren, and headed out. Annie, who wouldn't eat stolen oranges, had just ripped off a cop car.

Dave looked around him and wondered which way to go. The thought of jail scared him. Nothing was worse than being locked up and helpless, with people bossing you around and making you feel like scum. He remembered those old movies where the crook shouts out, "I'd rather die than go back there." Dave understood that. Jail scared him, but death didn't. Not really. What was so fantastic about being alive anyway?

If there had just been a way to die without any pain or hassle, if you could just reach up and flip a switch, then dying wouldn't be bad at all. But things didn't work that way. There probably wouldn't be anybody left alive if it were that easy.

Dave wasn't about to turn himself in, but he couldn't think of a decent plan. For a minute he thought of heading for the wilderness and living off the land. But that was movie stuff. What would he do for food? In the movies there were always wild berries and roots that the hero just happened to know about. More lies.

"Forget it," Dave said aloud. Even jail was better than starving to death.

He had to go back and try to find Annie and Jeff—not because they were his family but because they had some money and food and all the gear.

It took him a long time to pick his way through the scrub oaks and manzanita. When he crossed the final hill and looked down at the trailers and tents in the

campground, he relaxed a little. It was good to be
back on familiar ground. Maybe together they could
work out something. Maybe there was a chance.

He made a wide circle and came up on their campsite from the rear. He stopped and stared at the
empty space, feeling as lonely and empty as he had
ever felt.

"Dave," Annie whispered.

Dave almost smiled. He should have known better.
Anybody else in the world would have had sense
enough to grab the goodies and run. But not Annie.

"Are you okay?" she asked him.

"No problem," he said.

"Hey, it's the track star," Jeff said, moving up beside them. "So far today we've run from the cops and
stolen a police car and been shot at. What's next?"

"You'd better sit down and rest a minute, Dave,"
Annie said. "You look beat."

Dave lay in the shade while Annie wrote a letter
that their father probably wouldn't get. Nobody
could tell that to Annie, though.

He kicked off his shoes. Somewhere out there a
deputy was looking for him, but he felt safe right
then. "Hey, Annie," he said, "where'd you leave the
car?"

She kept writing. "Up the road."

He looked over at her, wanting to say something
more. But what? "That's good," he mumbled.

IV

On his way to the White Bar Store, Jeff stayed off the road wherever he could. Even though he was wearing a different shirt and a bathing suit, he figured Scotty would recognize him right away. But one of them had to go to the store to mail Annie's letters and buy groceries, and he was the obvious choice. Even Annie had accepted that.

Jeff jogged the final quarter mile, looking over his shoulder every few steps. Only one car, a dusty Volkswagen, sat in front of the store. Jeff glanced up and down the road, then pushed open the door. Darby was bagging groceries for a woman with a baby on her arm.

Jeff hurried down the aisle and picked up seven packages of spaghetti, seven cans of tomato sauce, a carton of salt, a can of stove fuel, and a box of oatmeal. He carried them to the counter while the woman was still trying to balance her groceries and the baby.

"And I need a map," Jeff said while Darby punched the register.

"What kind?"

"Like on the wall there," Jeff said. "The map for around here."

Darby nodded and brought out a map from under the counter. Jeff folded it twice so that it would fit into the grocery bag.

"Let's check the damage," Darby said, punching the register. Jeff held his breath as the total came up, but it was seventy cents less than he had. (Two points for Annie and her figuring.)

"And I need two stamped envelopes and a change of address card," Jeff said when the old man pushed the bag toward him.

Darby scooted his stool over to the post office window. He handed Jeff the change of address form, then dug into a drawer. "I hope you want big envelopes. That's all I got."

"That's fine. Do you have a pencil?"

Darby laid the envelopes and a pencil on the counter. Jeff filled in the form quickly. He could feel the old man's eyes on him. "Mr. Darby, do I have to put in the zip code on this?"

"That's the law," Darby said. "And you don't want to break the law, do you?" He handed Jeff a yellowed booklet. "Look it up in there."

Jeff found the zip code for Alder Creek and gave the form to Darby. Then he addressed the envelopes: one to his father at the Tok Junction address; the other to Mrs. Locke, in case his father changed his mind and came back to Cooperville.

Jeff dropped the envelopes in the mail slot and reached for the grocery bag. Darby leaned across the counter and grabbed Jeff's wrist. "You're flat nuthouse crazy," the old man said.

Jeff tried to pull free. "What're you doing?"

"You crazy kids think you can walk all the way to Alder Creek? Don't you know what that country's like out there?" He gave Jeff's wrist a jerk. "I'll bet you don't even have a compass."

"Let go," Jeff said, trying to ease backward. The old man's fingers remained clamped on his wrist. "What are you doing?"

"I'm trying to save your worthless hides." He yanked Jeff toward the counter. "You don't have a compass, do you?"

"No."

The old man snorted. "I figured. And you probably wouldn't know how to use it if you did. And I suppose the only shoes you got are those things you have on."

Jeff glanced down at his sneakers. "I'd better go now."

"You're idiots," Darby shouted. "You're gonna get yourselves killed." He reached into the bag and pulled out Jeff's map. "Take a look at this thing."

When Darby let go of his wrist, Jeff thought of grabbing the groceries and running. But they needed that map. He glanced out the window at the empty road and decided to give the old man one minute but to stay out of reach.

Darby spread out the map on the counter. "Take a look here. Once you get past Hooker Lake, there's no trail at all. You could spend weeks wandering around out there." He pulled a pencil from his pocket. "See this here?" He made a circle on the map. "This is Kendrick Peak. It's the tallest mountain you'll see. Anytime you get on high ground you'll be able to spot it. You keep that on your left-hand side the whole time. You'll be wanting to cross these mountains up here." He drew another line. "You paying attention?"

"Yessir."

"You better be. There's still snow up there, and you're gonna have a tough old time of it. You keep moving up this way." He drew a dark line on the map. "Now listen to me. You'll come up to three peaks. The one in the middle is sort of rounded off like an ice-cream cone. That's McGeorge Peak. You go on the left-hand side of that one." Darby's hand suddenly darted out and caught the front of Jeff's shirt. "Let me hear you say it."

"What?"

"What I just told you. Say it."

"Go on the left-hand side of the rounded-off peak."

Darby nodded and let go of Jeff's shirt. "Don't forget that. It's not as high through there, and you might be able to make it. I did it a few times years ago when I was a lot tougher and a lot stupider. If you get over the top, the rest isn't so bad. Just head downhill. Follow any creek you can. They all run into Brown Bear Creek sooner or later. You got that?"

"Yessir." Jeff moved back out of range of the old man's hands.

"Just stick with Brown Bear Creek. There used to be an old logging road on the west side, but I haven't been in there for twenty years. It's probably shot now. You just stay with that creek long enough, and you'll hit the highway. From there it's about two miles to the right to Alder Creek. Go left, and it's ten miles to Kirkland."

"Could I use your pencil?" Jeff scribbled "Turn right at the road" on the top of the map.

"You're a bunch of idiots," Darby said. "You don't know what you're in for." He yanked a cellophane package from a rack behind him and slammed it on the counter. "This stuff is moleskin. You ever heard of it?"

"No."

"I figured. When you get blisters—and you'll get 'em with shoes like those—cover 'em up with this stuff." He shoved the package into the bag and began folding the map. "And steer clear of anybody out there. Miners, dopers—they're all nuts. You see somebody, you run like crazy. And keep your food up high at night. Hang it from a tree limb. The bears won't bother you probably, but some of those idiots have been feeding the deer and turning them into camp robbers. So keep your stuff up out of their reach."

"Thanks for everything." Jeff reached for the bag.

Darby put his hand on the sack. "Tell your sister I said you'd be a lot smarter to turn yourselves in."

"I'll tell her."

Darby snorted. "She won't listen. You kids'll go ahead and do what you were gonna do anyway."

The door banged open. A man in shorts and a Dodgers T-shirt led a small girl inside. "We're out of marshmallows again," the man told Darby.

"I'm free," the girl announced to Jeff, holding up three fingers.

"Good for you." Jeff picked up his groceries and started for the door.

"Looks like we got company," Darby said.

A white sheriff's car pulled up across the road. Jeff

ducked down behind a rack of paperback books and eyed the car through the window. Scotty was behind the steering wheel, looking down.

The girl pushed a package of marshmallows up onto the counter. Her father slammed down cartons of soda and beer. Darby began tapping the register.

"What's your name?" Jeff asked the girl.

"Mary Elizabeth Carpenter," the girl announced. "I'm free."

"Are you camping?" Jeff asked her.

She turned to her father. "I want a marshmallow."

"Are you staying at the campground up there?" Jeff asked the girl's father.

The man nodded. "You don't need any more marshmallows."

The girl began to sniffle. "I want a marshmallow. Pleeeease."

Jeff glanced through the window. Scotty was opening the car door.

"You stop that right now," the man said.

"Excuse me, sir," Jeff said. "Do you think I could get a ride back to the campground with you?"

"Please, Daddy," the girl said. "I want a marshmallow."

"I said no, and I meant no." The man picked up the groceries with one hand and grabbed the girl's arm with the other.

"Would it be okay?" Jeff asked again.

"I guess so." The man sighed. Jeff held open the door for him.

Scotty was standing beside his car, talking to a man in overalls. Jeff hid his face behind his grocery bag and stayed close to the others. He climbed into the back seat and kept his head down until the car was

moving. When he looked back, Scotty was still standing in the same spot.

"I'm free," the girl declared from her car seat up
front.

Jeff leaned back and tried to remember everything
Darby had told him. Except for heading north and
staying to the left of some mountain, everything was
a blank just then.

Maybe when he got out the map, he'd remember
more.

Annie kept looking ahead of her, trying to spot a trail. The huge ponderosa pine trees blocked out the late-afternoon sun. Two thoughts kept creeping into her mind: It was getting dark, and they were lost.

From the time they had left Twin Lakes, the trail had been impossible to follow. They came to one fork after another and had to choose between faint paths running off in different directions. The meadows were crisscrossed with trails, all looking alike. Out-croppings of rock popped up where the trail disappeared entirely.

But they kept going, taking the easiest routes, and sooner or later came back to the main trail.

This time, though, they had been walking for a long time without stumbling onto the trail. Annie thought of backtracking, but she wasn't sure she could find her way back. Tired as she was, she trudged along and watched the ground in front of her. She didn't look around often enough to have a clear idea of the territory they were passing through. Besides, it all looked alike.

"Hold it," Dave yelled, and let his pack slip to the ground. "I've got to rest a minute." He sank down.

Jeff helped Annie lower her pack, then sat down beside Dave. Annie leaned against a tree.

"We shoulda stayed at Twin Lakes," Dave said.

"You know better than that, Dave," Annie said, keeping her voice calm. Twin Lakes had been crawling with campers.

"We shoulda stayed there," Dave said.

Jeff looked up and chanted:

> We shoulda done this.
> We shoulda done that.
> We shoulda gone after you
> With a baseball bat.

"We'd better not wait here too long," Annie said. "It'll be dark in another hour."

"I knew we couldn't make it all the way to Hooker Lake today," Dave muttered. "I told you that before we ever started. But you knew all about it."

Jeff leaned back and smiled at Annie. "Here's a new poem just for Dave," he said.

> Ho-ho-ho.
> I told you so.
> You never have to wait long
> For Dave to tell you you were wrong.

"Stuff it," Dave said without opening his eyes.

"Let's go on a little farther," Annie said. "We're headed in the right direction. Sooner or later we'll run across the trail again. What do you think, Dave?"

Dave didn't move. "Why ask me now?"

Jeff got to his feet. "Dave doesn't want to decide anything now. He'd rather wait and gripe later."

Dave pointed a finger at Jeff. "You keep that up, and you'll be saying all those cute little poems without your teeth."

"Let's go on a little ways," Annie said. She reached for her pack, but Jeff took it and slipped his arms through the straps. Annie checked her watch. If they didn't come across the trail in twenty minutes, she'd consider turning back.

From there on she tried to memorize the land around them so that they could backtrack if they had to. But it all looked the same—big pines in all directions. Except in the brushy canyons, only a few scrubby bushes grew between the trees. Walking was easy enough, once you got used to the slick needles, but each rise led to more of the same.

After twenty minutes Annie wasn't sure they could find their way back if they wanted to. It seemed smarter to push on and look for a camping place. "You want me to take that pack, Jeff?" she asked.

"I'm okay," he said. "I always stagger at this time of day."

In the middle of a small clearing, she found a tiny stream, maybe six inches across. The water was icy cold. "We'll stop here," she announced.

"Somehow I thought Hooker Lake would be bigger than this," Jeff said, slipping out of his pack. "I know. You don't have to say it. Shut up, Jeff."

Dave set his pack on the ground and lay down beside it. "I hurt all over."

Annie began to gather wood for a fire. She hoped the others would see what she was doing and help. She knew better than to give Dave orders.

Jeff was soon alongside her, breaking branches off the downed and rotting trees. They each carried several loads to the campsite before Annie scooped out a pit and started a fire. Dave lay in the same place, his eyes closed.

While Annie boiled water for spaghetti, Jeff studied the map. "I think I see the problem."

"Which one?" Annie asked.

Jeff laughed. "I wish I'd said that. Best line of the day. I mean the Hooker Lake problem. The case of the disappearing trail. We should have been heading just slightly northeast."

Annie looked over at him. "So?"

"Look where the sun went down. If that's west, then that's north." He pointed off to the side. "I figure we've mostly been going north, maybe a little northwest."

"You think we're far off?" Annie asked.

"Probably not. If we head straight east in the morning, we ought to run across the trail."

Dave opened his eyes. "Why didn't you figure that out ahead of time?"

"We'll be fine in the morning," Annie said. "Right now I just wish this water would boil. I'm getting hungry."

Somewhere above them an owl hooted. Annie shuddered, then forced herself to smile when Jeff turned toward her.

"This camping expedition is brought to you by good old Grace," Jeff said. "I hope I see her again sometime, so I can thank her properly." He scooted closer to the fire.

Grace, Grace,
I hate your face. . . .

VI

Dave crouched close to the fire but couldn't get comfortable. The biting cold crept up his back while his front baked. His blistered feet stung, and his whole body ached. The spaghetti sat like cement in his stomach.

"We might as well get into our sleeping bags," Annie said. "It's the only way to get warm. What makes me mad is that I left my coat at Mrs. Locke's. Middle of summer—who would have thought about cold?"

Jeff stood up and turned his back to the fire. "Would you like to hear my poem about spaghetti?"

"No," Dave told him.

"I know you don't mean that," Jeff said.

> I'm always ready
> For a plate of spaghetti.
> I'm easy to please.
> I'll take it with sauce or with cheese.
> But it doesn't taste as good
> When you're lost in the wood.

"Please, please. No applause. It embarrasses me."

"We're not really lost," Annie said.

They used their hands to sweep up mounds of pine needles. They spread the sleeping bags on the mounds, smoothing out lumps and filling in low spots. Dave crawled into his bag and decided that the work hadn't been worth it. "It's still a crummy bed," he muttered.

"It doesn't matter," Annie said. "I could sleep on concrete tonight."

While Dave tried to find a comfortable position, he kept thinking about stories he had heard of bears mauling campers. The way his luck was running, he'd better be careful. He hoped there was plenty of wood to keep the fire burning.

For a long time they lay in their bags and watched the fire. Every once in a while one of them would reach out and toss on more wood. Jeff was the first to go to sleep. Dave looked over his sleeping brother to see if Annie's eyes were still open. They were.

Dumb. That's what she was. His sister was so dumb it was incredible. Just because the deputy had been about to run him down, Annie had jumped into the car, set off the siren, and blasted off down the road. Now she was in worse trouble than he was.

He wasn't going to take the blame either. He hadn't made her hop into that car. If she was in trouble, it was because of her dumbness. It was stupid to mess yourself up just to save somebody else. But that was Annie's way. She was always trying to make things better, to fix things. She was too dumb to know that there were a lot of things that just couldn't be fixed.

But she *had* kept him out of jail. They were up

here in these ridiculous mountains where they'd probably die, but he wasn't in jail. He glanced toward her and thought about saying thank you. She'd eat that up. He wouldn't even have to explain. Just "Thank you" would do it. But he didn't say it. She was probably asleep by then anyway.

Dave slept in bits and snatches. He would wake up cold and aching, toss some sticks on the fire, and then settle back into a half doze again. Toward morning he jerked awake from a dream in which the deputy, carrying a TV set in his arms, was chasing him through the White Bar Store. Dave reached out and set several limbs onto the coals. While he waited for the wood to catch, he heard a shot, then two more.

Jeff sat up in his bag. "What was that?"

"Gunshots," Dave said. Two more shots crackled off to their left, the echoes sounding in the canyons.

"Must be hunters," Annie said. "Probably after a coon or something."

Three more shots sounded: two quick ones followed by a pause and then another shot.

"If they're hunters, they're lousy shots," Dave said.

They sat and stared out at the darkness. The only sound was the wind in the pine branches.

After several minutes Jeff crawled far enough out of his bag to toss another branch on the fire. "Boy, does it get cold up here at night."

"These have to be the crummiest sleeping bags in the world," Dave said.

They watched the fire blaze up and listened for more shots. "What time is it?" Jeff asked after a while.

Annie held her watch toward the fire and said,

"Almost four-thirty. It'll be getting light in a little while."

They settled back into their bags. Dave reached out and added one more stick to the fire before shutting his eyes. He crouched into a tight ball and listened. The fire popped and sputtered, and overhead the branches groaned in the wind. Once he thought he heard somebody yell.

He was suddenly aware of noises that weren't the fire or the wind. Footsteps crunching through pine needles, growing louder all the time. Dave opened his eyes and turned toward the sound. "Somebody's coming," he whispered.

"I hear it," Jeff said.

Dave reached into his jeans pocket for his knife. He opened the blade and gripped the handle.

"They're coming right toward us," Jeff said.

"It's the fire," Annie whispered. "They must have seen our fire."

The crunching footsteps grew louder, and a figure became visible in the firelight. It moved awkwardly, in a sort of sideways shuffle. Dave turned his knife so that the blade lay flat against his wrist, hidden from sight.

It was a man, running with his left arm hanging loose and his right arm across his chest. "There's something wrong with him," Jeff whispered.

The man ran straight toward them. He was wearing a powder blue down jacket with a dark spot on the shoulder.

"What do you want?" Dave called out.

The man stopped beside the fire, looked around, then dropped to his knees next to Dave's sleeping bag. "Help me!" he pleaded.

Dave slid forward slowly, still holding his knife blade hidden. The stranger's face, partially covered by his stringy blond hair, was young. Tears dribbled down his cheeks and onto his beard.

"Oh, Lordy, I'm dyin'." He slumped sideways.

Dave reached out to steady him and felt the sticky wetness. "He's bleeding!"

Annie scrambled across Dave's sleeping bag. "I want to get his jacket off." She unsnapped the jacket, but when she tried to pull it away from the left shoulder, blood poured out.

"Get me something for a bandage," Annie shouted. Jeff ran to a pack and came back with Dave's T-shirt. Annie held the shirt against the wound. "What happened to you?" she asked.

"I been shot," the stranger said, sounding puzzled.

"How'd it happen?"

He looked at her as if he didn't understand. "Got some water?"

Jeff grabbed a cup and filled it from the stream. The stranger took the cup in his shaking right hand. Before he could drink, the cup slipped from his fingers and went clanging to the ground. Jeff refilled the cup and held it to the stranger's lips.

"Get me some more stuff for bandages," Annie said. "This one is about soaked through."

Dave watched Jeff rummage through the packs and come back with another of his shirts. He realized that since Annie had taken over, he hadn't done anything but stare. He stood up and put away his knife. This fellow didn't look like a threat to anybody. But it was a weird business.

Dave stepped around Annie and looked down at the stranger. "Who are you anyway?"

The stranger took a minute to form the words. "Name's Cracker."

"What's this all about?"

Cracker shook his head and looked at Annie. "Oh, Lordy, I never had nothin' hurt like this before."

"Just take it easy," Annie said. "I think we're getting the bleeding stopped."

Dave leaned over and said, "Hey, Cracker, what's this all about? How'd you get shot?"

Cracker closed his eyes and didn't answer. His body began to tremble.

"We're going to slip off your jacket," Annie told him. "Then we can wrap it around you." She looked up at Dave. "Give me a hand here. I'll hold the bandage in place while you just ease this thing off. Try not to move his arm any more than you have to."

Dave tugged at the sleeve of the jacket, which was sticky with blood. Under the jacket Cracker was wearing a plaid shirt. Wrapped around his middle was a blue nylon daypack. Dave pulled the jacket free and draped it around Cracker's shoulders. Then he rinsed his hands in the stream.

"You see that?" Jeff said. "A light."

Cracker jerked his head around. "Where?"

"Across that way," Jeff said. "There. You see it that time?"

"I see it," Dave said.

Cracker pulled away from Annie and scrambled to his feet. He took one step forward, then swayed to the left and dropped to his knees. Annie caught him and eased him back to the ground. "Oh, Lordy," he said, "everything went black there." He glanced out at the darkness, then back at Annie. "You gotta help me. They'll kill me."

Dave knelt down beside Annie. "What's going on?"

"Those guys are gonna kill me."

"What for?"

Cracker shut his eyes. "Just help me. Please."

"Forget it," Dave said. "We're not getting mixed up in something like this. You better get up and get moving."

Cracker reached out and gripped Annie's arm. "We had us a little poker game, and I won all the money. Then those guys got real ugly. I tried to sneak out, and they shot me."

Dave stood up. "And you expect us to go up against some guys with guns? Forget it."

"We can't just let him get killed," Annie said, helping Cracker to his feet. "Come on. You can make it."

"Oh, man, everything is goin' around an' around."

"Those lights are heading this way," Jeff said.

"You'd better get moving," Dave said.

Cracker took two steps away from the fire, then grabbed Annie's shoulder. "I'm beggin' you. Help me."

"He can't do it," Annie said. "He can hardly stand up. We'll have to hide him."

Dave glared at her. "You're nuts."

"Quick," she said. "Move Jeff's sleeping bag, and dig out a space in the pine needles." Dave knew it would be useless to argue with her. He and Jeff clawed at the mound of needles, pulling it apart until there was a bare spot between two new mounds. Annie helped Cracker lie down in the space, then threw Jeff's sleeping bag over him.

"That won't work," Dave whispered, pointing at

the bulges in the sleeping bag. "Let's just tell them where he is."

Annie grabbed his arm. "You think they're going to leave three witnesses behind? Now come on. Maybe if Jeff gets in the bag, it won't be so obvious. And we can move our bags in close too."

The three of them kicked and clawed the other mounds of needles into a central pile, then threw the sleeping bags on top.

Annie let out a sigh. "All we can do is get into our bags and act like we don't know a thing."

"The blood," Jeff said. He ran over and began kicking dirt onto the red puddles.

"Throw the rest of the wood on it," Annie said.

They threw the wood into a new pile, then hurried back to their bags. Dave could hear Cracker moaning as Jeff climbed into his bag.

"This guy's not much of a mattress," Jeff said.

"We've got to make this look as natural as possible," Annie said. She moved Jeff several times before deciding that he'd have to sit up.

"Are you sure?" Jeff said.

"It's all right," Annie told him. "We'll all sit up. After all, if we hear shots and then see somebody coming, we're bound to be sitting up."

They sat and watched the lights come closer. A strong white beacon moved back and forth, probing the trees and bushes. Another weak yellow light bounced along with a steady rhythm.

"What do we tell them?" Jeff whispered.

"We'll say he came running past," Annie said. "They may find blood around here, so we can't just say we haven't seen him."

"I'll do the talking," Dave whispered.

"Let me," Annie said. "They're more likely to believe a scared girl."

The lights came nearer. Footsteps crunched toward them. Two men stopped at the edge of the clearing and looked around before moving forward into the firelight. They were dressed like Cracker, in down jackets and jeans. One man stayed close to the trees. The other, a tall, thin man with a shaggy black beard, came straight toward them. The bottom of a leather holster stuck out below his jacket. "Did a guy come by here?"

"Yes," Annie said. "He came in close, then went on past. We didn't get much of a look at him. He was running funny. Kind of bent over."

The man glanced around quickly. "Which way did he go?"

"Right out that way." Annie pointed into the darkness.

"How long ago?"

"I don't know. Ten or fifteen minutes, I guess. Maybe more."

The man turned and trotted off into the darkness, his light bouncing as he ran.

"What's going on?" Dave asked when the other man moved closer to the fire.

"I hate to scare you," the man said, "but I don't have much choice." He ran his hand over his neatly trimmed beard. "You were really lucky he passed you by. I'm afraid he's dangerous."

"Dangerous?" Annie asked, her voice almost a squeak. Dave hoped she wasn't spreading it on too thick.

"He's psychotic. He'll be doing just fine, and then

something will set him off. He tried to kill us tonight. Maybe you heard the shots."

"They woke us up," Annie said.

"He's my little brother. I thought it would be good for him to get outdoors for a few days. He was all right until tonight. Then he had a nightmare, I think, and that got him going. I just hope we can find him and get him calmed down before he hurts himself." He studied them for a long minute. Dave wished he had thought to take out his knife. "This is a funny place to camp."

"I know," Annie said. "We were on our way to Hooker Lake, but we got a late start and then got off the trail somewhere. Finally it got dark, and we were stuck. Do you know where the trail is from here?"

"You're about a mile from it," the man said. "But if I were you, I'd go back to Twin Lakes. If you'll go right back down this canyon and follow the creek downstream, you'll get there with no trouble. It's the smartest thing to do right now. I hate to think of you out here with my brother running loose."

"We'll do it," Annie said. The man turned away and seemed to be looking at the ground near the woodpile. "What should we do if we run into him?"

The man looked back at her and shook his head. "I'd keep as far away from him as you can. If he comes after you, scatter. He may seem all right, but he's unpredictable. I just wish I'd never brought him out here."

"Maybe we'd better get up and start packing," Annie said.

The man nodded. "I think it'd be a good idea. It'll be light before long." He started away from the fire.

"Sorry, kids. It's too bad your camping trip got messed up."

They sat and watched the light move off into the trees. When it disappeared over the rise, Jeff moved to the side and pulled the sleeping bag away. "You all right?"

Cracker sat up slowly. "I guess. Still kinda dizzy."

Dave studied the fellow's blond hair and red face. If he was the other man's brother, then Lucky Bates was the pope. Both of them were liars—Dave was sure of that. "All right," he said. "You're in the clear now. Take off."

"Listen here," Cracker said, "I've got to get this shoulder fixed. You people got any bandages?"

Dave threw a stick on the fire. "If we had any bandages, you wouldn't be messing up my T-shirt right now."

"I gotta do somethin'," Cracker said. "I gotta take care of this thing, or I'm gonna bleed to death."

Annie started to speak, but Dave cut her off. "You do whatever you want. Just do it somewhere else. We saved your hide once. Now it's up to you."

Cracker stood up and took a few awkward steps away from the fire. When one foot tramped into the creek, he swayed and seemed about to fall. Annie started toward him, but Dave stepped into her path. "Let him be."

"Dave, we can't—" she began, then shook her head.

Cracker, his foot still in the water, reached into his pants pocket and drew out a roll of bills. "I'll give y'-all a hundred dollars if you'll do somethin' for me."

Dave grabbed Cracker's arm and led him back to the fire. "Let's hear it."

"There's a first-aid kit back at the cabin where I was stayin'. I want somebody to go get it for me."

Dave stared at the roll of bills. "And get ourselves shot? Forget it."

"There's nobody back there. Those two'll keep lookin' for me all night. It's just a little ways. You can make it there an' back in ten minutes. Please. I need your help." He lifted the fistful of bills. "An' I'll pay for it."

"We'd better get packed up," Annie said. "We can't stay here, no matter what." She began stuffing things into a pack.

"Give it a try." Cracker set the roll in his lap, peeled off a bill, and handed it to Dave. "Here's fifty bucks. If there's any problem, forget the whole thing and keep the fifty." He lowered himself to the ground beside the fire. "It's just a little ways. You bring that kit back, and I'll give you another fifty." He looked up at Dave. "What do you say, partner?"

Dave stared at the bill in his hand. "Where is this place?"

Using Cracker's flashlight, Dave and Jeff trotted through the trees. Every few minutes they stopped, flipped off the light, and searched the darkness. If they saw one beam of light anywhere, Dave was going to forget the whole thing.

The directions Cracker had given them were clear enough. They had left the creek at the big boulder and headed straight uphill until they hit a path. Anybody who could give directions like that had been around the area quite a while. One more proof the other creep was lying.

Dave figured they were all crooks and liars. He

wouldn't turn his back on any of them. But there was a fifty-dollar bill in his pocket. And that was something you could trust.

They moved into the meadow Cracker had told them about. "We must be getting close," Jeff whispered.

Dave glanced behind them. "Maybe."

They crossed the meadow until they reached a creek, then followed it upstream until they saw the cabin sitting in a stand of trees. "Just like he said," Jeff whispered. "Let's get that kit and get out of here."

Dave studied the dark cabin. He wondered what else those liars had inside. If Cracker was flashing fifty-dollar bills, they might find something more interesting than a first-aid kit.

But, as usual, things weren't so easy. The door to the cabin was padlocked, and the windows on the left side were boarded over. "I'm glad we got the fifty ahead of time," Dave said.

The windows on the other side were uncovered but locked tight. "Get a rock," Jeff whispered. "We can break out the glass."

"Forget it," Dave said. "If the back's no better, we'll take off. That creep can bleed to death for all I care."

High up on the back wall was a single window, a narrow opening covered by a screen. Jeff stood on Dave's shoulders and tried to work the screen loose.

Dave hoped the scraping and scratching noises weren't as loud as they seemed. "Hurry it up," he whispered.

Jeff slid back to the ground. "I got it loose. I think I can squeeze through there. I want to put this flashlight in my pocket. I'm going to need both hands to pull myself up."

"Let's do it," Dave said. "We've been here too long already." He stood against the cabin and held his hands out for Jeff's first step. Jeff moved from Dave's hands up onto his shoulders. Dave gripped his brother's ankles to steady him.

"Okay," Jeff whispered. "When I say 'shove,' give me as much of a boost as you can." Dave heard more scraping and scratching. "Shove." Dave pushed the ankles as high into the air as he could reach. When he let go, the feet disappeared upward.

A moment later Jeff's head appeared in the window. "Keep an eye out," he whispered. "Tap on the house if there's anything funny."

"Just hurry," Dave said. He felt his way along to the corner of the cabin. He had trouble finding his footing in the dark. He wondered if it was worth the effort to go all the way to the front of the cabin. Jeff wasn't going to be inside that long.

Dave held his hands out in front of him and moved a few steps away from the cabin. He figured that he had a partial view of the front, but it was hard to be sure in the darkness. He wished he had gone to the other side, where the windows were. He could have seen the glow from Jeff's light at least.

Some kind of animal scurried through the leaves. Dave wondered if it was a rat. He wouldn't mind a squirrel or chipmunk, but rats were different. He wasn't going to move another step, maybe step on a rat's tail and have it turn and sink its teeth into his leg. Or maybe the rat would panic and race up the legs of his pants. He had seen that in a movie once.

Disgusted with himself for being so silly, he went ahead and tucked his pants legs into his socks.

He wondered what was taking Jeff so long. Cracker hadn't been sure where the kit would be, but the cabin wasn't that big. Jeff should have been able to cover every inch of it by now.

Dave squatted down. He was really beat. After all that walking he'd had almost no sleep. He felt like a zombie.

The first sounds he heard were footsteps. He jerked up, expecting to see Jeff. But the footsteps were in the wrong place. They were in front of the cabin. Then he heard a metallic click and the creaking of hinges.

Somebody had come back to the cabin. And Jeff was still inside.

VII

The door rattled. Jeff turned and stared. The lock snapped. He looked at the bedroom doorway, clear across the room. It was too far. He snapped off the flashlight.

Could he make up a believable story? What if he said the wounded one had threatened to kill Annie if he didn't get the kit? But would he even get a chance to talk? Those two might shoot him the second they spotted him.

The door creaked open. Jeff slid under the table and crept toward the wall.

He had been done in by applesauce. After digging through mounds of dirty clothes and muddy gear, he had finally located the first-aid kit in the bottom of a pack. But instead of clearing out, he had come back over to the table, planning to grab some of the freeze-dried applesauce that was lying around.

Wedging himself between the stumps that served as table legs, he thought of Annie and all her lectures about stealing. Why hadn't he listened?

And what in the world had happened to Dave?

Somebody stepped into the cabin. Jeff heard the scrape of a match, and the room was suddenly lit. He watched a pair of boots move across the floor toward the table. Then a man swore, and the light disappeared. A minute later another match was lit, and Jeff could hear banging and scraping just above him. A paper bag landed on the bench, a foot from his head. On the third match the man managed to light the lantern, and the whole cabin was bathed with wavering white light. Jeff began to eye the half-open cabin door. He wondered if he could scoot across the floor before the man could pull his pistol and fire it.

For a minute the boots stayed in one spot beside the table. Jeff wondered what the guy could be doing. Then he heard the scratch of another match and smelled the rotten sweetness of marijuana smoke. The boots moved across the room and stopped beside the pack where Jeff had found the first-aid kit.

It was the man who claimed to be Cracker's brother. Jeff was relieved. This one seemed less scary than the other. But he still had a pistol on his hip.

The man threw the pack aside. Jeff wondered if he had been looking for the first-aid kit. The man pawed through a pile of clothes, swore quietly, and looked around him. Jeff didn't move. If he could see the man, the man could see him—if he glanced that way.

The man walked back toward the table. Jeff felt himself relax as the man's head and shoulders disappeared from sight. The light flared up and then dimmed. Jeff realized the man had picked up the lantern. Several foil envelopes slid off the table and plopped to the floor. The man swore and kicked one

of the envelopes. It smacked against Jeff's leg. Jeff
glanced toward the doorway but stayed still.

The boots turned and headed for the bedroom. Jeff
crept out from the wall. As soon as the man stepped
into the other room, Jeff crawled across the floor and
dived out the open doorway. He slid down the rough
steps, scrambled to his feet, and tiptoed forward.

He waved his hands in front of him. After the lantern light he couldn't see anything. His fingers
smacked a tree before he saw it. He put the tree
trunk between himself and the cabin and stopped to
get his bearings.

A hand clamped over his mouth, pulling him backward. He sank down, his heart pounding in his chest.

"Take it easy, turkey. It's me." Dave pulled him
farther back into the trees before letting him go.

"Oh, man," Jeff whispered.

"Let's get out of here," Dave said.

"I can't see much," Jeff told him. "My eyes aren't
used to the dark yet."

"Just follow me," Dave whispered. "We've got to
get moving."

Jeff crept along behind Dave. He thought of holding onto Dave's belt. He didn't do it, but he stayed
close enough so that he could have.

When they stopped to drink at the creek, Jeff had
recovered enough to ask, "What happened anyway?
How'd that guy get past you?"

"How should I know?" Dave said. "He didn't have
a light or anything. I don't know where he came
from."

"That's the last time you'll be a watchman for me."

"Don't give me that. You think I wasn't scared too?
I was out there with my knife, ready to charge in and

take him on." He bent down and took one last drink. "What were you doing in there anyway? You know how long you were gone?"

"Let's get moving," Jeff said. Dave was always right. Even when he was wrong. Especially when he was wrong.

VIII

Annie sat on the ground, her back against a tree. Beside her lay Cracker, breathing rapidly and groaning. It was almost daylight. She could make out the trees around her. And if she could see, she could be seen.

A rustling in the leaves sent her sprawling to the ground. She lay flat, studying the land around her. Even when she spotted a squirrel pawing under a bush, she stayed where she was. The way their luck had been running, she wasn't about to take any chances.

Cracker twisted sideways and moaned.

"Shh," Annie said, sitting up.

His eyes snapped open. "Are they back?"

"Not yet."

He started to pull himself up, then winced and settled back. "How long they been gone?"

"Almost an hour."

"They shoulda been back already."

"Cut it out," Annie said. "I'm scared enough without that kind of talk."

"Sorry."

Annie looked down at his thin face and matted beard. She wondered how old he was. Eighteen maybe. Twenty at the most. "What kind of name is Cracker anyway?"

He shrugged and shifted his weight, clenching his teeth as he moved. "It ain't the way I thought."

"What do you mean?"

"My shoulder. You see it on TV, and you think you know what it's like to be shot. But it's different than you think."

"Does it hurt a lot?" Annie asked.

"Oh, Lordy, you betcha. But it's not just that. It makes you sick too. I feel like I ain't slept for a week an' just ran forty miles besides. I'm so tired I can't get my head straight."

"You'd better rest then," she said.

He nodded and closed his eyes again.

Annie spotted Dave and Jeff before she heard them. They were trotting through the trees by the creek, fifty yards below her. She stood up and waved her arms.

They rushed up the hill and sat down on either side of her. "Good thing you waved," Jeff told her. "We would have gone right on by."

"Things look different in the daylight," Dave said.

Jeff looked over at Cracker. "How's he doing?"

Annie rocked her hand back and forth. "He's been asleep most of the time."

"Lucky devil," Jeff said.

Dave nudged Cracker's knee. Cracker jerked and

then groaned as he opened his eyes. "We got your kit," Dave told him.

Cracker's face twisted as he pulled himself up to a sitting position. "Thanks," he whispered.

"Forget the thanks," Dave said. "We want our fifty right now."

Cracker nodded and pulled a fifty-dollar bill from his jeans pocket.

Dave grabbed the bill and set the kit beside Cracker. "All right. Let's get out of here."

Cracker looked past Dave and caught Annie's eye. "Could you fix my shoulder before you go?"

"Forget it, sucker," Dave said, hoisting his pack. "We're out here in the open, and it's getting light. There's no way we're hanging around."

"Help me up?" Cracker reached out toward Annie. She set down her pack and pulled him to his feet. Cracker swayed as he took two steps over and leaned against a tree.

"Get your pack, Annie," Dave said.

Jeff helped her into the pack. "I'll take my turn later."

"Look here," Cracker said, "there's a patch of willows just a little way up the draw. We'll be hidden there. Will you just come that far with me an' fix up my shoulder?"

"Forget it," Dave said.

Annie started forward. "Come on, Dave. We need a safe place to eat anyway."

"Dumb," Dave muttered. "Just plain dumb." He turned to Cracker. "Well, go ahead then. Show us where this place is."

Cracker swayed as he walked, but he kept moving.

The others followed him along the hillside, glancing around as they went.

Once they were in the middle of the willows, Annie felt safer. Dave kept watch at the edge of the thicket while Jeff fired up the stove.

Cracker shrugged his jacket off and lay down. Annie pawed through the kit. She didn't know much about doctoring. She found a container of iodine, told Cracker what she was going to do, then began working iodine into the wound.

Cracker bit into his jacket, his head quivering. He raised his feet off the ground and madly kicked at the air.

After a while she made him turn over so that she could work on the shoulder from the back. The wound was wider and messier on that side. Annie gagged once, then gritted her teeth and slopped iodine onto the torn flesh. Cracker bit into his jacket.

By the time Annie finished bandaging the shoulder, Jeff had the oatmeal ready. Annie took her bowl from him, not sure she could hold anything down. The three of them ate in silence. Cracker lay on the ground, apparently asleep.

Jeff finished his food and set his bowl aside. "That guy's got the right idea," he said. He lay down and curled into a ball.

"Don't go getting comfortable," Dave told him. "We're heading out right away."

Annie pointed at Cracker and looked at Dave questioningly.

"Bye-bye," Dave said.

Annie moved close to Dave and whispered, "You think we should just go off and leave him?"

"You bet," Dave said. "We've got problems enough

without him. I don't know what's going on with that
bunch, but we don't need any of it."

Annie glanced back at Cracker. "I wonder why
they shot him."

Dave set down his bowl. "I couldn't care less."

"It just seems wrong—" Annie began.

"Forget it," Dave said. "Leave the sucker."

"All right." She gathered up the breakfast things,
wiped them off as best she could, and stuffed them
into her pack. When they were ready to leave, she
knelt beside Cracker and whispered, "We're leaving
now."

"No. Please." He reached out toward her. "Don't
do that."

"We have to go."

Cracker pushed himself up to a sitting position.
"Listen, wait till tonight and help me get to White
Bar. I'll give you another hundred dollars."

"I'm sorry."

"Please. I need your help. If you don't want to wait,
that's okay. We can go now. Just go slow and let me
stay back out of sight."

"We're not going to White Bar," Annie said.

"I don't care. Wherever you're goin', take me
along. Just get me back to the highway, an' I'll give
you a hundred bucks."

Dave came back toward them. "You just had to go
and wake him up, didn't you?"

"Hey," Cracker said, "I'll give you another hundred if you'll get me out of here."

Dave shook his head. "You're on your own, sucker.
We've got things to do."

"Just let me follow along behind you. You won't
hardly know I'm there. I won't get close or nothin'.

Just get me to the highway. It's the easiest hundred bucks you'll ever make."

"We're not going that way," Dave said. "Annie, get your pack."

"You got to," Cracker said. "It's the only way outa here—unless you're fixin' to head right up over the mountains." Annie could feel his eyes on her face. "Oh, Lordy, that's what you're doin', ain't it? You're goin' over the mountains."

Dave glared at Annie.

"I didn't tell him a thing," she whispered.

Dave turned to Cracker. "Look, sucker, it doesn't matter where we're going. You're not coming with us."

"I wouldn't be no trouble," Cracker said.

Dave turned away. "Forget it."

Cracker reached into his jeans and drew out the roll of bills. "There's five hundred dollars here. Take me along, an' it's yours. Just get me outa here."

Dave glanced at Annie, then at Cracker. "Five hundred?"

"That's right. Five hundred bucks."

"It's crazy," Dave said. "We got a lot of miles ahead of us. Messed up like you are, you'd never make it."

Cracker smiled. "That's my problem, good buddy. If I die, you get the money all the same."

Dave took Annie aside. "Let's take him," he whispered. "If he slows us down too much, we can always dump him. But five big ones would make things a whole lot easier when we get to Alder Creek."

"I just wish I knew what was going on," Annie said. "What's a kid like him doing with a roll of bills like that?"

Dave shrugged. "Who cares? We can sure use it."

Annie walked back to where Cracker was standing. "Who *are* you?"

"They call me Cracker. I told you that."

"You know what I mean. We want to know what's going on here."

Cracker shook his head. "No, you don't. The less you know, the better. Just get me outa here an' take the money an' forget you ever saw me."

"Sounds good to me," Dave said. "Let's move."

Before they left the willows, Annie used Cracker's belt to make a sling for his arm. He ground his teeth each time she adjusted the belt. "You going to be all right?"

"Who knows?" he said.

"Give us a little start," Dave told Cracker. "We don't want you with us—ever. If we run into your pals, we don't want to have to explain what we're doing with you."

"Doesn't matter much." Cracker slid his daypack around to his hip and opened the zipper. Smiling, he pulled out a long-barreled revolver and waved it in their direction. "If they catch us, you can say I forced you to help me. Said I'd shoot you if you didn't. They can't argue with that."

"Careful with that thing," Annie said.

"Don't worry, sister. I'm always careful." He pointed the revolver at their feet. "You get the picture? I didn't have to ask. I could have made you take me with you." He winked at Annie. "But I don't like workin' that way. I'd rather keep things strictly business." He smiled and shoved the pistol back into his pack.

IX

"Hold up," Annie said. "Cracker has to rest."

Jeff looked back to where Cracker lay stretched out on the ground. "We just rested."

Annie slid her pack off her shoulders. "Give him five minutes."

Disgusted, Jeff sat down on a rotting log. He was plenty tired, but he wanted to get as far away from that cabin as possible.

They were still in pine forest, the ground open beneath the trees except for fallen limbs and occasional clumps of scrubby brush. Because of the trees, they couldn't see more than a hundred yards in any direction. If they hadn't been following the creek, they might have ended up walking in circles.

He got out his map and tried to locate their position. The short-bearded guy had said that they could get back to Twin Lakes by following that creek downstream. They were heading upstream, so they were probably traveling north, more or less. But he

had no idea how far they had come—except that it
wasn't far enough.

About two o'clock they stopped to cook some spaghetti. Cracker lay down in an open spot and fell
asleep immediately. The others sat and waited for
the water to boil.

"We're so dumb," Annie said. "We should have
gotten some salami and stuff we didn't have to stop
and cook."

Jeff studied the map again. "The rate we're going, I
figure we ought to make Alder Creek by Halloween.
Or Thanksgiving anyway."

"We're doing all right," Dave said.

Jeff turned toward him. "This old walk-two-min-
utes-and-rest-ten business gets to me after a while."

"For five hundred bucks you can put up with it,"
Dave said.

Annie snapped the spaghetti in half and dropped it
into the water. "I wonder where that money came
from."

"Don't worry about it," Dave told her. "When you
go into the store and slap down a bill, nobody cares
where it came from."

"Just think," Jeff said. "Some kids my age join Boy
Scouts so they can go out and do this for fun." He
shrugged when nobody responded. "You want to
hear another poem about spaghetti?"

"No," Annie said. "I don't want to hear a poem
about anything. I just want to rest a minute and have
something to eat and get as far from this place as we
can."

Jeff lay back on the ground. "You're the boss, but
it's your loss."

After lunch they began a slow, steady climb. The

pine forests began to be broken up by patches of rocks, where only a few scrawny bushes grew. The trees were smaller, and Jeff could spot the mountain peaks around them. It was harder than he expected to match up the peaks he was looking at with those on his map.

As the country grew more rugged, they often ran into a barrier of rocks or a sheer drop-off and had to backtrack. Jeff moved out ahead of the rest to scout for the best path. He was always nervous when the others were out of sight, but several times he saved them from dead ends.

Whenever he had a minute, he would stop in the open, spread out the map, and try to decide which mountains were which. Then, when the others got close, he would fold the map twice and stuff it into the back of his pants. It was too much bother to fold the map small enough to fit into a pocket.

Around four o'clock he had left a stand of Douglas firs and was heading uphill toward a rocky point. From there he hoped to get a view of the entire mountain range. The others were still back in the trees, probably resting again. Since they had started climbing, Cracker had been stopping more often.

Jeff was surprised by the intensity of the sun. Heat waves rose from the rocks in front of him. Squinting his eyes against the brightness, he marched forward. Maybe up ahead he could find a spot with both a view of the mountains and a little shade.

"Hold it!"

Jeff stopped in mid-step. The short-bearded man moved out from behind a boulder. He held his pistol straight out in front of him, aimed at Jeff's head.

Jeff stared at the pistol for a second, his whole body

trembling. He realized that he had to act immediately.

"Don't shoot!" he screamed as loudly as he could. "Oh, please, don't shoot me! I'm just a little boy!" He fell backward onto the ground. He hoped the map wouldn't slide out of his pants. "Oh, please, don't kill me!"

"Shut that up." The man shoved his pistol into its holster.

Jeff wished he dared to scream again. He could only hope the others had heard. He pulled himself up into a sitting position and scooted back against the rocks. "Please don't hurt me, mister."

"Nobody's going to hurt you. Just settle down."

Jeff started to speak, then broke into a sob. He was surprised when tears actually started down his cheeks.

"Settle down," the man said. "What are you doing here?"

"Trying to get home." Jeff's voice cracked. "Last night you said we could get to Twin Lakes if we followed the creek, and I've been following it and following it."

The man groaned. "Downstream. Not upstream. How old are you?"

Jeff wondered how far he could squeeze it. "Ten." When the man glanced at him, he added, "Almost eleven."

The man shook his head, started to say something, then shook his head again. "Where's the rest of your bunch?"

"We got split up. Your brother came after us." Jeff began to cry again.

"When was this?"

"This morning. We were just getting started. He came out of some bushes, and we scattered." Jeff used his sleeve to wipe his eyes. "He came after me, and he wouldn't quit. He kept saying he wouldn't hurt me. But I didn't let him get close. He couldn't move very fast. There was something wrong with him."

"Where was this?"

"Down by where we camped. He followed me for hours and hours. Then he fell down by the creek and didn't come after me anymore."

"When was this?"

"I don't know. Couple hours ago, I guess."

"It was this creek down below here?"

"Yeah. I've been staying with it the whole time. You think your brother's dead?"

"No, he's probably just resting. He'll be all right. Now get up from there. If you hustle, you can be at Twin Lakes before dark."

Jeff stood up slowly. He reached back and shoved the map all the way into his pants.

"What are you doing?" the man said.

"Huh?"

"What are you doing with your pants?"

"Nothing."

The man's eyes narrowed. He started toward Jeff. "I saw you. You were doing something."

Jeff broke out sobbing. "It's not my fault," he wailed. "You scared me so bad with that gun that I did it in my pants."

The man groaned. "Really?"

"I couldn't help it," Jeff said. "Now I'm all messed up."

"Come on." The man passed Jeff, shaking his head

as he glanced at Jeff's pants. Jeff followed slowly, making no effort to keep up with the man's long strides.

"Hurry it up," the man called over his shoulder.

Jeff began to sob again. "It's not so easy to walk. I'm all messed up and everything."

As Jeff followed along, he glanced around him, hoping Annie and Dave had managed to find cover. Then he spotted them. Twenty feet below, somebody's blue jeans were sticking up above a rock. It had to be Dave. It was just like him to crouch behind a rock and leave his rump sticking up in the air.

Jeff hurried forward. The last thing he wanted was for the man to turn around again. Nobody could miss that mass of blue twice.

Trotting past, Jeff tried to signal for Dave to get down, but that patch of blue didn't move.

When the man did look back, Jeff ran toward him, shouting, "I'm trying to hurry. I really am. I'm trying as hard as I can."

The man gave Jeff a disgusted look and started forward again.

Once they had passed through a stand of firs, Jeff slowed to a walk. When the man stopped and glanced back, Jeff was fifty yards behind. "Hurry up," he yelled.

"I can't," Jeff wailed. "My pants are all messed up."

"Then shut up that whining and go down to the creek and clean yourself up. But hustle. If you'll get a move on, you can make it back to Twin Lakes before dark. Your people are probably all waiting for you there. But don't fool around. You don't want to be out here overnight, do you?"

"No," Jeff called. "I'll hurry."

"Then quit standing there, and go do it."

Jeff cut straight down the hill to the creek. As he came near the water, he glanced back and saw the man watching him. Jeff unhitched his belt, then stepped behind a boulder. When he looked up a few minutes later, the man was gone.

Jeff plopped down beside the stream until his arms and legs stopped shaking. Then he took a long drink. He scrubbed his face in the icy water before heading back uphill.

He had only gone a short distance before he saw Annie waving. He headed toward her, keeping an eye on the spot where the man had disappeared. She ran up and hugged him tightly. "Thank goodness you're all right."

Jeff grinned. "I'm okay, except for the ribs you broke just now." He looked over at Dave. "Listen, Dave, don't give me that look. I had to play young and dumb. I didn't really mess my pants."

Dave laughed. "I don't care if you *did*. You handled him just right. I was sure he was going to spot us. Cracker here had his gun out, but he was so shaky he probably would have shot himself."

Cracker, who was sitting a few feet away, didn't seem to hear.

"Let's move," Jeff said. "He may start wondering what happened to me."

"I don't think he'll be back for a while," Annie said. "But you're right. The sooner we get out of here, the better." She reached down and helped Cracker to his feet.

"Maybe I'd better take that pistol," Dave said to Cracker. "You couldn't do anything with it if you had to."

Cracker put his hand on his daypack and turned away. "Don't bet on it, good buddy."

They headed away from the creek, crossing a series of rolling hills. Jeff led the way, avoiding open spots whenever he could. Cracker moved more and more slowly. Without saying a word, he would collapse onto the ground. The others would squat down and wait. Annie would allow him ten minutes, then pull him to his feet.

Just before sundown they stopped in a small meadow beside a noisy stream. Even though the spot seemed well hidden, they decided against a campfire.

"I'm too tired to gather wood anyway," Jeff said. He filled a pot with water while Annie set up the stove and lit the burner.

Cracker stretched out on the grass and didn't move again. When the spaghetti was finally ready, Annie looked in his direction. "What about him?"

"I don't think he's hungry," Dave said.

They were too tired to eat much. When they were finished, Annie woke Cracker and got him to take a few bites. Then he drank a cup of water and settled back onto the ground. "Long day," he said.

Dave pulled off his shoes and examined his feet. "Oh, man, my feet are like hamburger."

"Look like hamburger, smell like Limburger," Jeff said.

"Stick them in the creek," Annie told him. "The cold water should help."

Dave stuck a foot into the water and howled. "I don't know which is worse," he said, "the cold or the stinging."

"It doesn't look like much fun," Jeff said, "but I'd better do the same."

The three of them sat side by side, dangling their feet in the water. "Just think of all the streams we're polluting right now," Jeff said.

Afterward, they put Darby's moleskin over the worst of the blisters. Then they slipped their socks back on to warm their feet.

"What about you?" Annie asked Cracker. "How are your feet?"

"My feet ain't my problem," he said.

"I wish we had a sleeping bag for you," Annie told him.

"There's a blanket in the first-aid kit," Cracker said. "It's in a little-bitty package."

Jeff found the packet and opened it. The blanket seemed to be made of heavy tinfoil, but from the writing on the package, he figured it was probably warmer than his thin sleeping bag. "I'll try this tonight," he said. "Cracker can use my bag." He rolled up in the crinkling blanket and wondered if he had made a good choice.

"How is it?" Annie asked him after getting Cracker settled.

"Like rolling up in a newspaper," Jeff said. "Only not quite so warm."

"Get your bag back from Cracker then," Dave said.

"I'll see." Jeff was too tired to move just then.

Jeff awoke suddenly and tried to shift around for a comfortable spot. The blanket kept him warm enough, but it offered no padding at all. He rolled onto his side and pulled his knees up against his chest.

As he began to drift off, he heard stomping in the brush. He sat up and looked around. The stomping continued, maybe fifty feet away. He slid out of his blanket far enough to make sure that Annie and Dave were still in their bags. When he heard Cracker moan, Jeff began punching Dave's sleeping bag. "Hey," he whispered. "Hey."

Dave came scrambling out of his bag. "What's the matter?"

"There's something out there," Jeff said.

"Oh, no," Annie said.

Dave listened, then crawled toward Cracker. "Cracker, wake up."

"What? What?" Cracker said out loud.

"Get out your pistol," Dave whispered. "Somebody's out there."

"Keep it quiet," Cracker said. "Let's see."

They listened for several minutes. Jeff was afraid that nothing was going to happen, that they would think he had been dreaming. Then the stamping noise came again, even closer than before. Cracker snapped on his flashlight and moved the beam in that direction. Two eyes reflected the light. "Stupid deer," Cracker said.

Once Cracker said that, Jeff could make out the deer's outlines in the light. The deer looked up and snorted but didn't run away.

"Thank goodness," Annie said.

"Those things are a real pain," Cracker said. "People feed 'em stuff, an' pretty soon you can't get rid of the dumb things. They'd walk right into our cabin if we didn't keep the door shut."

"I think they're neat," Annie said as a second deer moved into the light.

Cracker laughed. "If we were a little farther away from those guys, I'd shoot one. They're good eatin'."

"Don't you dare," Annie said.

"Don't worry about it." Cracker snapped off the flashlight. "You'd better gather up all your food. Those buggers'll get into anything."

"Gimme the flashlight," Dave said.

"Sweet talker, ain'tcha?" Cracker said, but he handed over the light.

They stuffed the food inside the packs, then moved them in close to their bags. The deer continued to graze in the meadow. When Dave threw a rock in their direction, they trotted away, then stopped a few yards farther on. They watched Dave for a minute, then began to browse again. Dave threw another rock and chased them out of sight.

"Maybe you could hit one between the eyes and stun it," Jeff said. "Then you could run up and cut its throat."

"Maybe you could—" Dave began, then stopped and climbed into his sleeping bag.

Soon everything was quiet. Jeff straightened his blanket and tried to get comfortable.

Cracker struck a match. Jeff turned to watch him light a cigarette. The stink of marijuana filled the air.

Annie sat up in her sleeping bag. "What are you doing?"

"I need a little medicine, sister. "I'm hurtin' bad."

"Get rid of it," Annie shouted.

"Settle down, Annie," Dave said. "What's the big deal?"

"It's good stuff, woman." Cracker drew in smoke and was quiet for a minute. "I'd offer y'-all a hit, but I only got a little, an' I need every bit of it."

"We don't want your filthy pot," Annie said.

"That's good."

"If I'd known you had that stuff," she said, "I'd have left you back there this morning."

Cracker didn't say anything until he lay down again. "Oh, Lordy, I don't know if I'm gonna live through the night. An' I don't know if I want to."

X

"What a crummy day," Dave muttered as he unrolled his sleeping bag. It was Sunday evening, and
they were still in the middle of nowhere. Yesterday
the mountains had been looming directly in front of
them. Only one last canyon had stood in their way.
But they had spent the whole day crossing that canyon.

The climb down was bad enough—picking their
way through the trees, retracing their steps to go
around cliffs, then fighting their way through thickets to reach the stream.

But coming out of there was worse. That side of the
canyon was rock and scrub brush. They had to scram-
ble from boulder to boulder or fight their way
through thick brush when the boulders were too far
apart. Steep as the canyon was, they had to zigzag
back and forth, sometimes making a long loop only to
find themselves back where they started.

Cracker kept stopping, sinking to the ground and
refusing to move. If it hadn't been for the money,

Dave would have been happy to leave him where he lay. Back on Friday morning $500 had seemed like a lot of money. Now Dave figured they had already earned it—and more. If he'd had it to do over again, he would have left Cracker behind to bleed to death. For three days they had hauled that sucker along, helping him over the tough spots and listening to him moan. Dave was sick of it.

Cracker even griped about having oatmeal for lunch. It never occurred to him that they wouldn't be running short of food if he weren't there gobbling down everything he could get hold of. Five hundred bucks wasn't enough.

Dave glanced over to where Cracker sat huddled by the fire. The creep never lifted a finger around camp. While the others unpacked and started dinner and gathered wood, Cracker just lay around and whined. Tonight, once the fire was going, he got up and moved next to it—his big effort of the night.

"It's cold up here," Cracker muttered to nobody in particular.

"It's even colder when you're not scrunched up to the fire," Dave said, spreading out another sleeping bag.

Annie looked up from the stove. "We're pretty high—just a little way down from the timberline."

"I think I see where we are," Jeff called. He was sitting in an open spot, his map spread out in front of him. "We're a little east of where we're supposed to cross."

Dave wandered over to Jeff. Ignoring the map, he stared up at the two mountains that hovered over them. "Forget that map, and use your eyes. You see the dip between those peaks, don't you?"

"Sure," Jeff said, "but I'm pretty sure that the one on the left is McGeorge Peak. Darby said we're supposed to go on the other side of that."

"And you want to walk who knows how many extra miles because of what some old goat told you? What's the matter? Didn't you get enough hiking today?"

"If you two are feeling lively enough to fight," Annie said, "go find some more wood. We'll need all we can get tonight."

Jeff tapped his finger on the map. "Take a look at these contours. The pass on the other side of McGeorge Peak is several hundred feet lower."

Dave didn't look at the map. "And for a few hundred stupid feet, you want to walk a bunch of miles? What kind of sense does that make?"

Jeff shrugged. "All I know is what the map shows and what the old guy said."

"Well, get your nose out of the map and take a look. We can run straight up this ridge. Then we can cut over, across the snow, to the top of the pass. We'll be on the other side by noon. What's wrong with that?"

"It may not be as easy as it looks," Jeff said.

Dave snorted. "Nothing ever is."

"Annie," Jeff called, "what do you think?"

"I think we need some more wood," she said.

"We're heading right up there tomorrow morning," Dave said. "We'll be on the far side before noon."

Jeff folded the map. "I hope you're right."

Dave turned and looked down at him. "We're gonna try it. And if it doesn't work, I don't want to hear about it. Understand?"

Jeff grinned. "Would I say 'I told you so' to my big

smart brother? You bet your cotton-pickin' life I
would."

Dave wandered off and picked up a few pieces of
deadwood. He had an uneasy feeling that the little
snot knew what he was talking about. He always
seemed to. And then Dave would end up looking
dumb again. But it didn't make sense not to try it.

He carried his wood back and tossed it onto the
pile. Annie looked up from the stove. "I think I'll
cook up some extra oatmeal in the morning. That
way we won't have to stop and cook in the middle of
the day tomorrow."

"You figure you can gag down cold oatmeal?"

Annie nodded. "I can do a lot of things if there isn't
any other choice."

"Can you answer a question without preaching a
sermon?" Dave turned his back on her and settled
down beside the fire.

They picked their way uphill, zigzagging back and
forth between outcroppings of rock and little stands
of stunted brush. The wind blew down from above,
sharp with the bite of snow. Off to the side they could
hear crashing water, but the banks were too steep for
them to get close to the stream itself. From above, it
was a spectacular sight—waterfall after waterfall,
white water roaring down the mountainside.

Dave looked at the water disgustedly. Their canteen was almost empty. They could stand and look at
all that water but couldn't get close to it. He looked
above and saw the spot where the stream emerged
from a field of white. It was hard to believe that all
that water was coming from a patch of snow.

"Don't worry," he said, although nobody had spoken. "We'll be in the snow in a little while. Then we'll have all the water we want."

They moved upward, Cracker hanging behind as usual. Dave kept an eye on him. Sometimes Cracker would just quit and lie down. Then they'd go back and find him flat on the ground, his eyes closed. If he wasn't asleep, he was putting on a good fake.

When they reached the edge of the snow, Dave stopped and looked out across the glaring whiteness. "Hard to believe it's July," he said. The snow brought back memories of snowmen and snowball fights and coming inside afterward to drink hot chocolate.

He brushed away the top layer of dirty snow and scooped up a handful of ice. It made his teeth sting but didn't help his throat the way he thought it would.

Cracker moved up to the edge of the snow, looked around, and collapsed onto the wet ground. "I'm beat."

It was his last time, Dave figured. Once they got out on the snow, at least that sucker wasn't going to be lying down and grabbing naps.

"Let's move it." He tramped forward, his feet crunching through the brittle crust.

Jeff trotted along behind, whipping an imaginary team of sled dogs. "Mush, you huskies. Mush."

After ten minutes Dave decided that the worst thing about walking on snow was that you never knew what to expect. You might hit slick ice right at the surface and go sliding, or you might sink up to your knees in slush. He found himself wincing with each step.

He tried to walk lightly to keep from breaking

through so often. It was easier for the others. They
followed behind him, stepping in his footprints.

He scooped up a handful of snow, squeezed it into
a small pebble of ice, then popped it into his mouth.
For the hundredth time he wished he had sunglasses.
He was walking along with his eyes open only a
crack, and still the snow was dazzling in front of him.
And it was hot. Sweat was trickling down his fore-
head, even though his feet were growing numb inside his soggy tennis shoes.

When he came to an outcropping of rock, standing
large and gray above the snow, he climbed up on it,
happy to be out of the snow for a minute. "I hate
snow," he said to Annie.

She pulled off her shoes and began to squeeze water out of her socks. "I wasn't sure my toes were still
there."

"Dashing through the snow," Jeff sang as he
climbed onto the rock, "in a one-horse open sleigh,
o'er the fields we go—" He stopped and looked at
them. "Swearing all the way," he finished.

Cracker stumbled up to the rock. "It's rough."

"You ought to try it with a pack," Dave told him.

The wind whipped around them, plastering their
wet clothes against their skin. Dave began to shiver.
"Let's move," he said. He looked above him, trying
to locate the place where they would go over the top.
It seemed as far away as ever.

After he left the rock, Dave could hear a rushing
sound that wasn't the wind. It seemed to come from
the snow beneath him. "You hear that?" he called
over his shoulder.

"There must be a stream underneath," Annie said.
"We'd better move back."

"We're all right," Dave told her. He tramped forward, listening to the growling. His left foot struck something solid just below the surface. Rock, he figured. He stepped ahead quickly with his right foot, but there was no bottom. He stumbled forward and landed on his face as his feet sank downward.

Snow caved in around him, splattering against his neck and shoulders. He jerked his body around. The snow gave way each time he put his weight on it. He kept clawing and kicking, almost swimming.

Snow covered his face. He couldn't see anything. He opened his mouth, and ice covered his tongue. He pawed and twisted and wriggled.

His hand broke free, out of the snow. He waved wildly, scattering the snow until his head was uncovered. Then he lay still and sucked in air.

Annie came rushing toward him, her hand outstretched. "Get back, you idiot!" he screamed. He reached out slowly, dug his fingers into the crust, and eased his body up. The snow beneath him began to give way again. He clawed at the ice around him. His legs churned against crumbling snow.

His hand smacked against something hard. He grabbed at it with the other hand, then yanked his body toward it. Behind him snow continued to crumble and disappear into a widening hole.

Dave hugged his rock and worked his legs out of the snow. He moved carefully, afraid that even the rock might collapse.

After resting for several minutes, Dave let go of the rock and crept back to where Jeff and Annie were waiting. "That was a good trick," Jeff said. "Let's see it again."

"Are you all right?" Annie asked.

"I'm just fantastic," Dave said. "My clothes are full of snow, and I almost died out there. I'm just jim-dandy."

Cracker was sitting on the outcropping where they had stopped before. He didn't look up when the others joined him.

Dave shook the snow out of his clothes. He couldn't stop his teeth from chattering. While they watched, the hole he had made grew larger and larger as snow collapsed and disappeared into the stream beneath.

Dave knew they should turn back. But he hated to quit after coming so far. "Well, we learned something," he said finally. "We'll have to stay away from those hollows. There's water running along there, just the way there would be if there wasn't any snow." He looked around, ready to pounce on anyone who said anything.

Nobody responded except Cracker, who muttered, "I think I'm dyin'."

When they began again, Dave tried to stick to high ground, but it was hard to tell what the ground beneath the snowpack might be like. He kept plowing ahead, always listening for the faintest rumble. The snow grew deeper; the ice crust, less reliable. Soon he was above his knees as he slogged along. He yanked each foot out of its hole, set it forward a few inches, and felt it plunge down through the snow again.

Annie moved up beside him. "Dave?"

"It's all right," he snapped back. "It's a little rough going right through here, but we'll make it." But he knew that he was wrong, that they weren't going to get to the top that day. Still, he smashed his way forward for another half hour before he finally turned and held up his hands. "Can't do it," he said. "It's too far up there, and the snow's just too deep."

"Let's head on back," Annie said. "We'd better get down out of this stuff and get a fire going. We're all freezing."

Dave kept watching Jeff. He knew that behind that blank face, Jeff was laughing at him, saying, "I told you so." Dave waited for even a hint of a smile, but Jeff turned away and started downhill without a sign.

They moved down the mountain, walking in their own tracks. Dave brought up the rear. He had fouled up again. No matter what he tried, it turned out wrong.

He stopped at the outcropping and stared out at the hole he had made. Little chunks of snow were still crumbling and disappearing. He wondered what would have happened if he hadn't managed to get back to the rock. Would he have drowned in the water below, or would he have suffocated beneath the snow? Either way it would have been over quickly.

What had made him struggle so hard?

Stupidity, he decided. Just plain old stupidity. He was too dumb to die when he had the chance.

XI

As soon as the eastern sky began to color, Annie crawled out of her sleeping bag and built up the fire. She was relieved when nobody else stirred. Right then she was too tired and too sore to guard her face or her tone of voice.

She was scared. Their food was running low, and they were still on the wrong side of the mountains. Because she did most of the cooking, she wasn't sure the others realized how bad things were. Or maybe they were pretending, the way she was.

Once the fire was blazing again, she examined her feet and smoothed down the old patches of moleskin. They would have to do. Moleskin, like everything else, was in short supply. She shivered as she pulled on her socks, which hadn't dried during the night. Her shoes were still damp and stiff from the cold. She loosened the laces and eased the shoes onto her feet, trying to keep the bandages in place.

The pan which she had filled with snow the night before now held slush. She set the pan on the stove, then checked their supply of oatmeal. They'd be plowing through snow today, so she'd fix full portions. Tomorrow they would start rationing.

She decided to wake Cracker and bandage his shoulder while the water was heating. She knelt beside his sleeping bag and looked down at him. Something had happened to him last night. After three days of staggering along and sleeping whenever they stopped, he had suddenly come alive. He had sat by the fire talking and shouting, disgusted when the others crawled into their sleeping bags. Annie wondered if the change was caused by some kind of fever. It couldn't be marijuana. He had run out of that the night before.

Cracker was anything but lively that morning. Even when his eyes finally opened, he didn't seem to see anything. Annie checked the shoulder. "The bandage'll last another day," she told him. "We're pretty short of tape right now."

"Suits me." Cracker slid back to the ground.

"Nope," Annie said. "It's time to get up and get moving." She nudged him with her foot until he dragged himself out of the bag.

Cracker grumbled while he used his good hand to pull on his socks and boots. Before Annie could come and tie his shoelaces, he grabbed his daypack and headed into the brush.

"Breakfast in five minutes," Annie called.

By the time Cracker came back, Jeff and Dave were rolling up the sleeping bags. Annie was stirring the oatmeal. Cracker smiled as he moved up close to the fire. "Gonna be a good day today."

"I hope so," Annie said.

"Hey, woman, you got a second to tie up my boots?
It's a little tough to do that on my own."

"Sure."

While Annie tightened the laces, he looked down
at her. "Mighty handy to have a woman around.
Makes everything a whole lot better." Annie reached
for his other boot. "Hey, sister, you ever been to
Mexico?"

"No."

"That's where I'm headed. After freezin' my tail
off up here, I want to get out there on that Mexican
desert and bake my buns in the sunshine." He let out
a high-pitched giggle. "How's that sound?"

"All right."

He reached out and ran his hand over her cheek.
"You got a real sunburn yesterday, you know that?"

Annie pulled back from him. "I know. It really
stings."

"That glare off the snow is pretty rough," Cracker
said. "There's some of that white stuff—zinc something—in the kit. That might help."

Annie tied the second boot and turned back to the
stove. "Why didn't you think of that yesterday?"

"Yesterday I was dyin'."

She looked up at him. "And you're not today?"

"Today I might make it." He smiled at her, running his eyes over her body. "Feelin' a little better."

Annie looked away. She decided she liked him better when he was sicker.

For several hours they trudged across the mountain. Jeff scouted ahead for the easiest path, leading
them in and out of the scrubby vegetation along the
timberline. After the first half hour Cracker quit talk-

ing and began falling behind once more. Dave plodded forward, keeping his eyes on the ground.

Late in the morning Jeff stopped them at the top of a rise. "This is it. We'll follow this little ridge up, then angle toward that slot up there." Annie glanced upward. All she could see was bushes, rocks, and snow.

"Look at the snow up there," Dave said. "This spot doesn't look any better than the other one."

"It can't be any worse," Jeff said.

Dave hoisted his pack onto his back. "What choice have we got?"

"I think things are going to work now," Annie said. "I have a good feeling about this one." She wondered if she sounded as silly to them as she did to herself. But then Jeff grinned at her, and she figured the pretense was worth it.

They stayed off the snow as long as they could. When the rocky ridge they were following disappeared into a snowfield, Dave gave his pack to Jeff and broke trail. He used a pine branch he'd picked up earlier to test the snow in tricky spots.

They moved upward, staying away from the dips which might mean a stream underneath. After Dave had sunk to his waist twice, they began to avoid the outcroppings of rock that stuck up through the snow. The outcroppings offered them a chance to rest in a dry spot, but the snow around the rocks was unpredictable.

Annie had smeared her face with zinc oxide, but it still burned in the reflected sun. She desperately wished for sunglasses, then laughed at herself. If she was going to wish for things, there was no sense stopping with sunglasses.

Behind her she could hear Jeff panting but still

mumbling some kind of song. The chorus was his old standard—"Grace, Grace, I hate your face"—but he seemed to have some new words.

At a little past noon Dave broke a path to a large outcropping so that they could stop and rest. Annie hauled the stove out of her pack. "I'm going to get us some real water. I'm tired of sucking on snow."

When the snow began to melt, she filled a cup and passed it around. They kept adding snow to the pot and drinking off the water.

"The water tastes a little funny that way," Jeff said, "but it sure beats chewing snow."

"We're going to make it," Annie said. "We're not far from the top."

"But then where'll we be?" Dave said.

When everyone waved away the cup, Annie offered to make a little oatmeal.

"Don't bother," Dave said.

"Not right now," Jeff told her. "But if you could come up with a burger or a pizza, you might be able to talk me into it."

"Let's get moving," Dave said. "I don't want to hear any of his dumb talk."

"How about a taco?" Jeff said.

Annie roused Cracker, who had curled up in a ball. "Who needs it?" he said.

An hour later they were at the top. After a final steep climb they were suddenly walking on a nearly level snowfield, and new mountains and valleys lay in front of them.

"Look," Dave said. "More of the same."

"We made it!" Jeff shouted. "Darby was right. It's all clear sailing from here."

"Clear sailing to where?" Dave said.

Cracker caught up to them, glanced around for a minute, then sank down on the snow. "I've had it," he said. "You're lookin' at a dead man."

"No more climbing," Annie said. "This next part should be a whole lot easier."

Dave shrugged. "We'll see."

"Maybe we can slide all the way down," Jeff said.

Dave turned away. "Maybe you can fly too."

Moving downhill was harder than Annie thought it would be. Dave tried to break a zigzag path down the mountain, but they kept sliding on the icy surface. Annie's first slide was exciting until she smacked down on her bottom with a bone-grinding crunch. After that she was more careful about her footing, but it didn't help.

They slid and fell and picked themselves up and sank to their waists and slid and fell. Dave broke a trail where he could, and the others tried to stay in his footprints. And the wind blew against their wet clothes.

"If I get out of this," Jeff said, pulling himself out of the snow again, "I'll never play in snow the rest of my life."

Sliding and slogging and tumbling, they moved slowly downhill. Hours passed. The wind grew stronger as the sun sank lower. Dave slid less often, and his trail grew easier to follow. Rocks began to stick up in the middle of the snowfields. Dave angled to the right, working his way toward a black granite ridge that rose out of the whiteness.

When Annie stepped onto the granite, she stamped her feet to knock the snow off her shoes. She stamped once more, just for the fun of it. "It's so nice to feel something solid."

Dave took back his pack and headed downhill. He didn't stop until they were below the timberline, surrounded by trees. There they gathered wood and built a fire.

Annie decided to fix half the spaghetti that was left. That wouldn't be enough to satisfy them, but it would leave something for the next day.

"I wish there was more," she said as she filled the plates.

"That's all right," Jeff said. "I've been thinking about going on a diet anyway."

Annie glanced over at Cracker, hoping he wouldn't eat. But he had his plate between his knees and was using his good arm to shovel in the spaghetti. He winked at her, and she looked away.

When the food was finished, Cracker moved off into the trees. He took his daypack with him as always. Jeff went uphill to get a pot of snow while Dave gathered more wood.

Cracker came marching back to the fire a few minutes later, his good arm swinging free. "Too bad we don't have a radio. We could use a little bit of music." He turned toward Annie. "You and me, we could boogie a little, warm ourselves up some."

"We could use a little bit of a lot of things," Jeff said. "I'd start with pizza, then—"

"Cut it out," Dave said. "How long do you figure it'll take us to get to Alder Creek anyway?"

"I don't know," Jeff said. "My map doesn't go that far."

Dave stared at him. "What do you mean?"

Cracker squatted down beside Annie. "What do you say, sister? If you feel like dancin', I'll just sing for us."

"Hush." Annie scooted away from him. "I want to hear this."

"My map ends just past these mountains," Jeff was saying. "But Darby said for us just to follow the creeks. All of them run into Brown Bear Creek sooner or later. Then there's supposed to be an old road on the west side of Brown Bear. That'll take us out to the state road a couple miles from Alder Creek."

"Sounds easy enough," Annie said.

Jeff laughed. "So does climbing over a little snow."

"But how far is it?" Dave asked him.

Jeff shook his head. "You tell me. Darby said it was about thirty miles to Alder Creek as the crow flies. How far have we come?"

"A hundred, at least," Dave said.

"I shoulda shot that deer the other day," Cracker said. "Then we'd be eatin' steaks right now."

"Right," Jeff said. "That's what I need right now—a Bambi burger."

"What happened to those things anyway?" Dave asked.

"They stay down in the low country," Cracker said. "Even dumb deer got too much sense to be trippin' around up here."

"What a joke," Dave muttered. "Here we are sitting here with all this money, and what good does it do? I saw a movie like this one time. This guy had a million bucks' worth of diamonds, but then he died of thirst out on the desert."

"We're not going to die," Annie said.

"Just keep thinking that," Dave said. He looked over at the others and shook his head. "It's crazy. We could starve to death with six hundred bucks in our pockets."

"Shoot." Cracker began to giggle. Annie turned and stared at him. That high-pitched giggle was a strange sound for somebody Cracker's size to make. "You don't know the half of it," he said. "Six hundred bucks. That's nothin'."

Dave snorted. "Listen to the big talker. Six hundred's just spending money to you, right?"

"You might be surprised." Cracker giggled again. "There's a whole lot in this world you don't know about, sonny."

Dave tossed a stick on the fire. "I know about big talk, sonny."

Cracker smiled. "Know it all, don'tcha? Look here." He reached into his daypack. Annie moved back a little, expecting him to draw the pistol. Instead, he brought out a plastic bag and waved it around. Annie wondered if he had been hiding food from the rest of them. "You know what this is worth? Fifty thousand easy. Maybe a hundred. So don't talk to me about your six hundred bucks."

"What?" Dave said.

"That slowed him down a little, didn't it?" Cracker winked at Annie. "See this stuff, woman. This is the real thing, the big enchilada."

"What is it?" Annie demanded.

"What do you think?" He waved the package in front of her.

"How should I know?"

"It's the real thing. Cocaine, sweetie. First-cabin stuff." He giggled again. "Ask the guy that knows."

"I can't believe it," Annie yelled. "That's what that

whole business was about? That's why they were chasing you?"

Cracker tucked the bag back into his pack and shut the zipper with a flourish. "You got it, sweetie."

"And I was feeling sorry for you," she said.

"Listen," Cracker said, "I been hurtin' bad."

"I want to hear it," Annie shouted, getting to her feet. "The whole thing. How'd it happen?"

"Just stay cool," Cracker said. "You want the straight skinny, I'll give it to you. Just don't get your bowels into an uproar."

"Let's hear it," Annie said.

Cracker laughed and scooted closer to the fire. "After the way you carried on about a little pot, I wasn't gonna say nothin'. Besides, I didn't want you to get any ideas. But we're all good buddies now, so everything's cool." He pointed to Jeff. "What about you? You cool?"

"I'm so cool I'm still shivering," Jeff said.

Cracker laughed. "You know the ugly guy back there? That was Victor. He's the one that talked me into coming up here. He had this big scam going. He was growing pot in all different places—little patches down in the canyons. Then he stayed in the cabin and played like a gold miner. Even if somebody happened to find a patch of pot, Victor was okay. He could lose a patch or two and still come out fine."

"I can't believe it," Annie said.

"But Victor got tired of pullin' weeds an' haulin' water, see. So he came down to San Francisco an' talked me into comin' back with him. He was talkin' big money, an' I figured I'd go for it. But then I got to wonderin' how much Victor was really gonna give me." He turned his back to the fire and giggled again.

"I mean, look at it. If Victor kicks me out with a few lousy bucks, I can't exactly take him to court, see?"

"Wonderful," Annie said.

"So then this uptown dude, Clean Gene, shows up, and I begin to get the message. It turns out that the whole scam is Clean Gene's. Victor's just workin' for him. I start seein' my piece of the pie gettin' littler an' littler. But Clean Gene is carryin' this big load of coke he's just picked up over on the coast. Well, my old man didn't raise any dumb kids. When I saw that coke, I knew it was my ticket to the world. After waitin' around all my life, I was finally gettin' my chance to go for the big one."

"So you stole it," Annie finished, "and got shot doing it."

"I made a bad mistake," Cracker said with another giggle. "I shoulda shot both those guys. Perfect chance. They were both sound asleep. But I figured I could just slip out with the goodies and be long gone before they woke up. I was gonna head for White Bar, see, an' take Victor's truck. But they heard me leavin'."

Annie glared at him. "And you got us right in the middle of that? So what if we ended up getting shot? You didn't care."

Cracker giggled. "Hey, take it easy, woman. I didn't have a whole lot of choice right then. But we made it all right."

"No thanks to you." She turned to Dave. "Have you heard enough?"

"What're you talking about?" Dave said.

Annie stepped around Jeff and stood over Cracker. "This is it, Cracker. We're finished right now. You take your stuff and clear out."

"Annie, don't be stupid," Dave said.

Annie whirled around. "Don't *you* be stupid. The last thing in the world we need is to get mixed up with this kind of stuff."

"You get too excited," Cracker told her. "We're doin' fine."

"It's your own fault, Annie," Dave said. "You had to go asking all about it. And now you don't like what you heard."

"He'd better get out of here right now," Annie shouted.

"Don't be so dumb," Dave said. "Nobody's going anywhere tonight."

"I don't want any part of this," Annie shouted. She knew that she should stop, but the words kept coming out. "I don't want his dirty money, and I don't want anything to do with him."

"She's just blowing off steam," Dave said to Cracker.

"Maybe I am," Annie yelled. "But if you don't think I mean every word of it, you've got another think coming. We may be poor, but we're not trash. We can hold our heads up with anybody. Let 'em look down their noses at us. We know better."

Cracker giggled. "Me, I'll settle for bein' rich trash."

"And it shows all over you." Annie turned to Dave. "That's what it's all about. We don't want to end up slime like that." She stamped away from the fire, rolled out her sleeping bag, and yanked off her shoes.

"So you got this stuff," Dave said to Cracker. "What do you do with it?"

Cracker smiled. "Listen, good buddy, before Victor got me up here, I spent a whole year in San

Francisco. I know the place inside out. I figure I could score this whole bag in twenty minutes. But I won't. I'll sell part of it to two or three of the big boys. Then, when they see how good it is, I'll see who offers me the best price for the rest." He giggled again. "An' then I'll disappear into the sunset like the Lone Ranger. Hi-yo, Silver, away!"

"A hundred thousand," Dave said.

"Why doesn't everybody shut up and go to sleep?" Annie said.

Cracker grinned and shook his head. "When that woman turns mean, she turns real mean, don't she?"

"You'd better believe it!" Annie shouted.

Jeff spread his blanket next to Annie's bag and pulled it around himself. "I don't think I'll have much trouble sleeping tonight. I don't suppose anybody would care to hear a good night poem?"

"You're right," Annie said. She twisted around and lay with her back to the fire. She was sure of only one thing: The first chance she got, she was going to grab Cracker's pistol.

XII

Cracker led Dave away from the fire. Dave kept staring at the bulge in the daypack while he thought about the things he could buy with $100,000. First would be a brand new pickup—green, with chrome rims and a tape deck and air conditioning.

"Listen," Cracker said, "what's she so fussed about?"

"Don't worry about Annie. She gets started on something, and she has a hard time letting go."

"What about you, old buddy? This cocaine stuff bother you too?"

Dave shook his head. "None of my business."

"But you wish it was, right?"

Dave glanced at Cracker. "I could figure out what to do with a hundred thousand."

Cracker giggled. "Yeah, I don't think that's gonna be too tough. You ever had this stuff?"

"Not very often." He wasn't about to admit he'd never been around cocaine before. "That's for rich guys."

Cracker smiled. "Well, I'm about to become a rich guy. You want a little snort?"

"That's okay." Dave didn't want to look stupid.

"It's good stuff. It'd cost you hundred dollars a toot on the street."

"I'll take the money," Dave said. "Nothing's worth that much."

"You're talkin' like a small-timer." Cracker glanced over at Annie and Jeff, then asked, "How far you figure it is to that town?"

"Not too far."

"Think we'll get there tomorrow?"

"If we push it." Dave kept his eyes on the fire. He wished Cracker would quit foxing around and get to the point.

"Look here, buddy," Cracker said. "I know we made a deal not to ask any questions, but I've got a lot ridin' on this. What kind of trouble are y'-all in anyway?"

"Who says we're in trouble?"

Cracker smiled. "Nobody's gonna come the way we did if they got any choice. So what's happenin'?"

Dave gave him a short version of their story. The only lie he told was that he had planned to hock the stolen TV.

"That sister of yours, she's somethin'," Cracker said, moving back toward the fire.

After they had sat and stared at the flames for a while, Cracker stood up again and motioned for Dave to follow him. "Look here," Cracker said when he stopped walking, "I got a bad feelin' about this. The cops know there's three of you. They just might have spread the word. Somebody sees all three of you walkin' around, they might just remember."

"Nobody'll be looking for us in Alder Creek," Dave said.

"Maybe." Cracker glanced toward the fire. "An' I got a bad feelin' about your sister too. She could make things real hard for me."

"She'll be all right," Dave said, not sure it was true.

"Look, good buddy, I got my whole life in this pack. I almost got myself killed for it already. An' I've been hurtin' bad ever since. You think these last days've been rough on you? Man, you had it easy."

"Oh, sure."

"I'm tellin' you, you don't know what I been through. I thought I was a dead man. I'm talkin' about real pain."

Dave shivered once and looked back at the fire.

"Look, this is my chance. I ran off from home when I was fourteen, an' I've been on the streets ever since. Georgia, Texas, California—it's all the same. I keep hustlin' an' scramblin' an' gettin' stepped on by the big boys. But now it's my turn to do the steppin'. An' I'm not about to blow it because your sister gets some wacky idea in her head."

"She'll be all right," Dave said again.

Cracker shook his head. "I got a bad feelin' about her. An' there's too much ridin' on this one." He looked over at Dave. "I'm tryin' to figure you out, buddy. Seems to me you've had a pretty rough go yourself."

Dave shrugged.

"Maybe you're tired of bein' shoved around. Maybe not. That's what I don't know. Some guys get used to havin' their faces shoved in the dirt."

"You gotta be kidding."

Cracker held out his hand. "Here it is, buddy. I got a deal for you. Take it or leave it. No sales pitch."

Dave glanced over at the sleeping bags, then moved closer. "Let's hear it."

"I could use you," Cracker said. "With this messed-up shoulder, drivin' might be a little tough. An' I need somebody to cover me. You interested?"

Dave tried to keep his face blank. "Depends."

"Here's the story. I can use you, but I don't need those two. I can make it without any of you, if it comes to that, but I figure you and me could work together easy. What do you think? You interested?"

"I'm listening," Dave said.

"Stick with me, an' I'll give you a quarter. That'll be twenty, twenty-five thousand. Maybe more. What do you say? You ready to go for the big one?"

Dave thought of the green pickup. "I'm ready."

Cracker reached out and gripped Dave's arm. "You an' me, good buddy. You're not gonna change your mind?"

"No way."

"Just one thing. I want to go tonight. I want to be sure an' make that town tomorrow."

"You mean leave right away? No sleep at all?"

Cracker moved backward, his hand disappearing behind him. "After tomorrow we'll sleep plenty. You still with me?"

Dave wondered if Cracker had his hand on the pistol. "I said I'd go for it, and I meant it."

"We'll rest for a little while. Once we're sure those two are sacked out good, we'll take off."

Dave smiled as he squatted beside the fire.

* * *

"Hold it," Cracker called out. "I'm just wore out. Let's stop an' wait for daylight."

"Suits me." Dave let his pack slide to the ground.

"It's murder this way. You got the flashlight, an' I'm just fallin' over things in the dark. We're supposed to share the light."

"You didn't like going first either," Dave said.

"You oughta get shot once. Then you'd know how it is. Go ahead an' roll out my sleepin' bag."

"Yes, sir," Dave said.

"Don't hand me that. You know I can't do it one-handed."

Dave untied the bag from the pack and spread it on the ground. "Anything else you want, sir?"

"I hope you get shot someday. Then you'll know what it's like. This thing's on fire. It's like havin' somebody stick you with a red-hot poker."

Dave kept his mouth shut as he rolled out his bag. He had to get along with Cracker—for a little while.

"I've had it, buddy," Cracker said. "Tomorrow we're gonna make it to that town, an' I'm gonna sleep in a bed. I can't take any more nights on the ground."

Dave crawled into his bag and shivered. "Suits me."

Exhausted as he was, Dave couldn't get to sleep. Cracker was snoring away, moaning with each breath. "Shut up!" Dave said, but the moans continued.

Dave scrunched and turned, wishing for a fire. His mind flashed back to Jeff and Annie. He had stuffed everything useful into his pack: the food, the stove,

the bandages, the canteen. He wondered if they'd
make it all right.

He stopped himself right there. That was sucker
thinking. Nothing was ever going to stop Annie.
She'd come right down out of the mountains, preaching a sermon all the way.

Besides, they were nothing to him. So what if they
all had the same worthless father? Dave knew better
than to swallow the lies about family—all that blood-
thicker-than-water crud. That was just one more trip
the world laid on you to keep you in line.

What did those two have to do with him? They had
shut him out years ago. He remembered all the times
when Annie would hug Jeff and listen to his dumb
poems. Those two were a pair, and Dave was the
outsider. He always had been. He had stayed with
them only because he was too young to go anywhere
else.

But now his age didn't matter. When he took his
new pickup down the drive-through lane at McDonald's and handed a fifty-dollar bill to the girl at the
window, nobody was going to ask how old he was.
With money you were the boss. When you talked,
people listened.

His time was coming, and nobody was going to
spoil it. Annie and Jeff would make it all right. If
things were a little tough, Annie had nobody to
blame but herself. She should have kept her mouth
shut for once.

Dave wished he could sleep a little, though. Maybe
he could if Cracker would just be quiet for a minute.
But Cracker kept on moaning and groaning, the way
he did when he was awake.

Cracker was a pain, but for 20,000 bucks Dave

figured he could put up with the whining for a few days. He'd had plenty of practice being around people who were pains. He'd stick with Cracker long enough to get the money. After that it would be good-bye and good riddance.

He didn't trust Cracker, of course. He knew Cracker probably wasn't planning to give him his share. But Dave had his own plans.

XIII

Dave and Cracker walked all morning, following one stream until it joined another and another. Dave tried to stay far enough ahead so that he couldn't hear Cracker's complaints. He had to keep looking back, though, because Cracker would just flop down on the ground when the mood struck him. Then Dave would slide out of his pack and rest. Once he actually fell asleep for an hour and still had to go back and roust Cracker.

The canyon walls around them grew steeper. Dave's backpack was heavy and awkward, making climbing tough. And Cracker, moaning about having only one arm, always needed help. Dave wished they still had Jeff to go ahead and scout out the easiest route. Again and again he and Cracker would head into dead ends—steep drop-offs or tangled thickets— and have to retrace their steps. And Cracker would always whine about wasting time, as if Dave were to blame.

Late in the afternoon the stream they were following joined another larger stream. Dave stood at the water's edge and looked up and down the new creek. "I'd bet anything this is the one we want." He bent down and threw water on his face. "We're gonna make it."

"Give me some water," Cracker said.

Dave looked up at him. "Get your own."

"I'm hurtin' bad. It's too hard to bend down."

"I'll bet you could make it if you really wanted to," Dave said. But he took a cup out of the pack and filled it.

Cracker drank two cups of water, then poured the third over his head and rubbed the water into his hair and beard.

"You want to rest awhile?" Dave asked him.

Cracker shook his head. "It doesn't do no good. As long as I'm hurtin', I might as well keep movin'. I just want to get clear outa this place."

Following the new stream, Dave was thankful for the roar of the crashing water, which drowned out Cracker's whines. Soon, however, they had to move farther uphill to get away from the willows that grew close to the water's edge. The walking was easier there, even if he had to listen to Cracker again.

"The way you were talkin' last night," Cracker was saying, "I thought we'd be at that dumb town by now."

Dave moved ahead quickly. The last thing he wanted right now was an argument. He climbed over a fallen log and onto a flat piece of ground. He took several steps on the level surface before stopping suddenly and looking around. He glanced at the bank on his left, then looked ahead and behind him. "Now we're cooking," he yelled.

Cracker, struggling over the log, turned half-closed eyes in his direction. "What're you squawkin' about?"

"We just found that logging road," Dave said. "We've got it made now."

Cracker looked around and began to smile. "Oh, Lordy, it's about time."

Dave laughed. "When I saw that big creek, I had the feeling we were on our way."

"Let's move it," Cracker said. "I don't want to spend another night out here."

"Suits me," Dave said. He began to whistle as he started forward.

The road had been abandoned long enough for small pines to have sprung up in the center. An occasional fallen tree blocked their way, and sometimes the road ended in a gully, a section having washed away over the years.

"Ain't exactly a freeway," Cracker grumbled as they climbed around a washout.

Dave just grinned. Now that they were sure of their direction, he didn't mind a little climbing. He was thinking once more about taking that green pickup down the drive-through lane.

After a half hour on the road Cracker sank down onto the ground. "Why don't you go ahead an' fix somethin' to eat? I'm about out of gas."

"Why don't—" Dave began, then stopped. There was no sense arguing now. He started the stove and put on a pan of water. When the water finally boiled, he dumped in the last package of spaghetti and stretched out on the ground.

"Dave," Cracker said quietly.

"Yeah?" Dave said without opening his eyes.

"Dave." Cracker's voice was louder.

Dave turned sideways and opened one eye. The pistol was pointed at his head.

"The easiest thing for me would be to kill you," Cracker said.

"What're you talking about?" Dave moved up to a sitting position. The pistol rose with his head.

"It's pretty simple, old buddy," Cracker said. "I don't need you, an' I don't trust you."

"Come on," Dave said. "I thought we were partners."

"Well, buddy, I'm fixin' to dissolve our partnership."

Dave watched the barrel of the pistol. "You can't just kill me."

Cracker smiled. "Sure I can. Nothin' to it. But I won't, if you do just what I tell you."

"Name it," Dave blurted out. "Anything."

"Listen to that boy." Cracker giggled. "He's all of a sudden ready for cooperation."

Dave tried to smile. "I'm easy to get along with."

Cracker's voice was tight and flat. "Start by takin' the strings out of your shoes."

"Sure." Dave reached down and untied his shoes. His hands were shaking, and he had trouble catching hold of the strings. "Anything you say." When he finally managed to pull the string out of the first shoe, he held it up. "Here you go. There's no need for any of—" He stopped when he saw the disgusted look on Cracker's face.

After Dave had removed his shoelaces, Cracker made him pull the string out of his sleeping bag. "Keep one hand on top of your head while you're doin' it. It'll take you longer, but it'll keep you from gettin' any ideas. Besides, then you can see what I've been puttin' up with."

"Here you go," Dave said when the string was clear.

Cracker kicked the sleeping bag out of the way without taking his eyes off Dave. "Now I want you to tie your feet together. Good and tight. Don't play any games with me. I can just shoot you anytime."

The cold eyes and the steady pistol convinced Dave to do exactly as he was told.

Once Dave's feet were tied, Cracker told him to take off his belt and roll over onto his stomach. "I'm gonna tie your hands. It'd be a whole lot easier if I knocked you cold first. If you move one inch, that's what I'll do."

Dave knew that Cracker would have to put the pistol aside. He lay still and waited for his chance. When the time was right, he would spring backward and dive on top of Cracker, aiming for that wounded shoulder.

The first thing Cracker did, though, was to loop the belt around Dave's wrists. Just as Dave started to move, the gun barrel rammed into his neck. "Don't even think about it, old buddy."

Cracker wrapped cord around and around Dave's wrists. When the wrists were tied, Cracker removed the belt. "Bend your knees," he said. "Bring your feet up to your butt." He lashed Dave's hands and feet together, then flopped him over onto his side, next to a small oak tree. "You just might go rollin' around an' gettin' into trouble, so we'll just do this." He looped the belt around Dave's ankle, then cinched it to the tree.

Dave was left lying on his side, his body forming an

awkard, painful triangle. He twisted slowly, trying to settle himself.

"Cut out that wigglin'," Cracker said. "I wasted too much time on you already. You give me any problems, an' I'll fix you good."

Dave lay still and waited. Cracker drained the water off the spaghetti, dumped in the last can of tomato sauce, then sat back and ate from the pot. When he was finished, he tossed the pot aside and took a long drink of water from the canteen. Then he reached for his daypack and brought out the plastic bag. He glanced toward Dave, who closed his eyes.

Dave kept his eyes shut. He didn't want to see Cracker, didn't want to see anything.

He felt a yank on his wrists. Cracker was looking down at him. "You might be able to get loose," Cracker said. "Never can tell. By then I'll be long gone anyway. I'm takin' along a sleepin' bag, but that's just for restin'. I'm not fixin' to sleep until I find me a bed." He nudged Dave with his toe. "A guy like you—who knows what you were thinkin'? You really figure I was gonna make you my partner? Or were you gonna jump me pretty quick? What about it? You figure you were gonna outsmart ol' Cracker?" He giggled and stepped back. "I'll be thinkin' about you when I'm lyin' in the Mexico sun an' sippin' piña coladas."

Cracker tossed a sleeping bag over his shoulder and started down the road. Watching him go, Dave had a sudden urge to yell at him, but he couldn't decide what to say.

Once Cracker was out of sight, Dave began to squirm and pull at the cords. The strings cut into his wrists and tore at his ankles, but he continued to yank and twist, expecting to break free at any moment.

More lies, he thought when he finally lay still. More stupid lies. And he was sucker enough to fall for them. In all the movies people wiggled around and got free. Or they broke a bottle or found something sharp to cut their ropes. More of the same old lies. He was tied tight, and there was nothing he could do about it.

Lying there on the ground, his shoulders aching from being pulled backward, Dave hated himself for his stupidity. Had he really planned to take Cracker's pistol and make a killing in cocaine? And those stupid dreams—cruising in the green pickup, slapping down a fifty-dollar bill at McDonald's. He had believed in them so much that he had run off and left Jeff and Annie in the middle of nowhere. He had taken the food, the stove, the canteen. He didn't even know if he'd left them any matches. He hadn't bothered to check.

Jeff and Annie had been alone for a day now. Had they kept going? Were they headed this way? Was it possible that they might come along and find him? Then he caught himself. That was just more stupid dreaming.

As he thought about Jeff and Annie, things began to come back to him—times he hadn't thought of for years: the three of them riding on his old bike, Jeff on the handlebars, Annie on the seat, and him standing up and pumping away with all his might; the three of them decorating a Christmas tree with paper chains made from newspapers, riding on the Ferris wheel at the county fair, making popcorn in the skillet, cooking trout over a campfire.

Dave began to cry. He couldn't remember the last time he had cried, but the tears came easily. He knew that he was going to die. The best he could hope for was a quick finish.

Dave awoke with a start. Something wet was brushing his face. He tried to reach up, felt the pain at his wrist, and then remembered what had happened. Again something wet brushed across his cheek. "Hyaah!" he yelled.

An animal bounded away from him. Deer. He spotted two of them, maybe another. One began pushing the metal pot around on the ground. "Get out!" Dave shouted. "Get!" Then he whistled. The deer backed away a few steps but returned as soon as he stopped.

After a time Dave quit yelling. It made his dry throat hurt more, and it didn't bother the deer. For the moment they were busy with the backpack anyway.

Dave was shivering with cold. He kept thinking of the sleeping bag that Cracker had kicked off to the side. Dave pulled against the belt that bound his ankle to the tree. If he could break that belt, he might be able to get to the sleeping bag and cover himself.

He jerked away from the tree, feeling the belt cut into his leg. He figured it was hopeless, but he strained and pulled until he was exhausted.

A deer came past him, its small, hard hoof stepping on his leg. "Go on," Dave said. The deer nuzzled his shirt, then licked his cheek. "Get out!" Dave screamed. The deer stepped back and snorted.

Again Dave hoped he would die soon.

XIV

Ants for me and ants for you.
We'll cook them up and have ant stew.

"You just get worse and worse," Annie said.

Jeff laughed loudly—too loudly. He had been jabbering like this all day. At first he had done it for Annie, to keep her from worrying about him. After a while he couldn't stop, even though he knew he was getting on her nerves.

When Annie woke him that morning, she was trying to be brave. "We have a problem," she said. Then she started to cry and hugged him. "Oh, Jeff, they ran off and left us."

Whenever Annie cried, Jeff had a hard time holding himself back, but he managed to say, "Good. I'd had about all of those two I could stand."

They spent the next hour swearing at Dave and Cracker, inventing new names when the old ones got tiresome. Annie quit first. Jeff held on for a few more rounds, then switched to singing.

Ten hours later he was still singing:

> Ants for me and ants for you.
> We'll start a fire and barbecue.

"This looks like a good place to camp," Annie said, setting down her pack beside the creek they had been following.

Jeff glanced at the grassy clearing, then up at the sky. "We could go for another hour. It's not going to take very long to fix dinner."

Annie smiled. "This is far enough for one day. We don't want to get too worn-out."

Jeff shrugged and went to gather wood. All day they had traveled at a slow, easy pace, resting often and drinking plenty of water. Annie had the idea that if they drank enough water, they wouldn't get hungry.

"Annie," he called, "you're not scared of catching up to Dave and Cracker, are you? They've got to be miles ahead of us, and there's no telling which way they went."

"I don't even want to think about them," she said. "Right now all I care about is us."

"I've been thinking about Dave," Jeff said. "I think he was adopted."

Once they had gathered plenty of wood, Annie arranged a mound of tiny dead twigs and bits of pitchy bark. Then she glanced over at Jeff. "Do you need that map?"

"I think we're off it," Jeff said.

"Maybe you could tear off the bottom. I only have

three matches, and I don't want to take a chance on wasting one."

So the bottom third of the map went for the fire, which caught easily. They sat in the grass and watched it pop and flare. Jeff spread out the rest of his map and tried to guess their position.

"The old guy said all the streams flowed into Brown Bear Creek, but this map doesn't go that far. I'm not sure, but I don't think our creek here is big enough to be Brown Bear. Maybe we'll hit it pretty soon."

"How far do you figure we are from Alder Creek?"

"Five or ten miles," he said, although he figured it was probably more than that.

"Maybe we'll make it tomorrow," Annie said. "The next day for sure."

Jeff tossed a stick on the fire. "You know, this kind of camping has lots of advantages. No dishes to clean, no menu planning. It makes everything a lot easier."

Annie jumped up. "Let's go wading."

"You're crazy," Jeff told her.

"It runs in the family." She pulled off her shoes.

Laughing and shouting, they danced around in the swift water. Jeff's toes ached from the cold, and his teeth chattered, but he felt better than he had all day.

Afterward they warmed their feet in front of the fire and watched the clouds above them turn orange and purple.

"You know," Annie said, "it's beautiful here. So quiet and peaceful."

Jeff smiled. "Yeah, but I'd trade it all for a noisy pizza parlor."

"Tell me one of your dreams," Annie said.

"I never remember them, except for the night-mares."

"I don't mean that kind. I mean something you wish for. And don't mention food, or I'll throw you in the creek."

Just then Jeff couldn't think of anything but a hamburger and fries. He rubbed his toes and stared into the flames. "Don't laugh, all right?"

"I won't."

"Sometimes I think of being on television. I'd be one of those guys who come on the talk shows and tell jokes for a few minutes. 'And now, ladies and gentlemen, here he is, the funniest man in America, Jefferson County Bates.' And I come trotting out with a mike, and everybody is laughing even before I say anything."

"You'll have to get some new jokes," Annie said.

"What about you, Annie? It's your turn. What's one of your dreams?"

Annie smiled and looked into the fire. "I don't know. I guess I don't have very many."

"Sure you do. Come on. I told mine."

Annie smiled and poked at the fire. "Oh, I don't know. Sometimes I wonder what it would be like to live in one of those nice new houses, with a fence around it, and little trees growing up that are going to turn into big trees someday. And all the walls are smooth and clear. No holes, no nails. Wouldn't that be something—to have a brand-new place? And a nice neighborhood where people said hello to you when you walked down the street."

Jeff smiled and said, "Yeah," but he thought that Annie wasn't much of a dreamer. As long as she was wishing, she might as well go for a mansion with a swimming pool.

When Jeff first felt drops on his face, he ducked under the blanket and tried to go back to sleep. A minute later Annie was shaking him. "Come on, Jeff. Get back under the tree."

Soon they were huddled in Annie's sleeping bag, with Jeff's blanket—the only waterproof thing they had—draped over them. No matter how they arranged the blanket, though, water kept dribbling down on them.

"The fire's out," Annie said. "I don't dare try to start another one with everything wet."

"Annie," Jeff said, "do you think someday we're going to remember this night and have a good laugh?"

"No."

"I don't either."

It was past noon before they left their campsite. Annie had used most of the map and the driest twigs they could find to start another fire, and they had spent the morning getting their clothes and sleeping bag dry.

Jeff felt awful. Yesterday he had been hungry. Today he wasn't sure he could eat anything—even if there had been something to eat. His stomach felt as if he had swallowed a huge helping of cement.

He was worried about Annie. She looked shaky, and she was avoiding his eyes whenever she could. To cheer her up, he tried to make up a poem about spending the night in the rain. He couldn't get past "Rain is a pain," though.

They traveled along the hillside above the creek, moving much faster than they had the day before. Once in a while Annie insisted that they move downhill for a drink, but they didn't sit by the stream afterward.

As the sidehill grew steeper and rockier, they were forced closer to the water's edge. Soon they were fighting their way through clumps of willows. Jeff thought of crossing the creek, but the other side looked just as steep.

"We could use a machete," he shouted as he emerged from a thick stand of brush. Seeing water on either side of him, he thought they had reached a bend in the stream. Then he realized that both streams were flowing in the same direction.

"Hey, Annie," he yelled. "Good news and bad news."

Annie stepped into the open. "Give me the good news first."

"The good news is that we've found Brown Bear Creek. That's got to be it."

Annie looked around, then smiled. "It must be. What's the bad news?"

"The bad news is that we're going to get wet." Jeff walked across the shrinking triangle of land to where the two streams joined. He looked up the new creek, trying to locate a place to wade.

"It'd be easier to cross our creek," Annie said.

"Yeah, but Darby said the road is on the west side."

"Too bad. This looks pretty deep."

"Let's go back upstream and look for a better place," Jeff said.

"Good," Annie said. "Maybe we'll get lucky and find a fallen log."

He looked at Annie and laughed. "Maybe. The way our luck's been running, I wouldn't count on it."

They moved alongside the stream, avoiding the clumps of willows whenever they could. "I hate this," Jeff said after a while. "Every step we take puts us one step farther from Alder Creek."

When they found a spot where the creek widened a little, Annie headed for the water's edge. "It's not going to get any better," she said. "We might as well get on with it."

They took off their shoes and tied them around their necks, then rolled up their pants.

"I was ready to go wading anyway," Jeff said, stepping into the icy water. "Ahh! Refreshing."

"Stay close to me," Annie shouted. "That way, if one of us slips—"

"He can pull the other one in," Jeff finished.

The water was even swifter than it looked, and deeper. Five feet from shore Jeff was in water above his knees. "I'm so glad I took the time to roll up my pants."

"Keep moving," Annie called out.

"I'm not sure I can." He stood with both feet planted, watching the water swirl around his legs.

"We've got to keep going," Annie said. "Hold onto me and move up."

"Maybe we ought to try somewhere else."

"We're already wet. Just hold on and take a step."

Jeff grabbed Annie's shoulder and moved one foot ahead, then the other. When he had both feet firmly on the bottom, he looked back at Annie. "Okay. I'm squared away. Now you come."

Annie took several quick steps, then set herself while Jeff moved past her again.

"It's kind of like leapfrog," Jeff said, his lower lip trembling from the cold.

"If you fall in, don't—" Annie said.

"Forget it," Jeff interrupted. "We're not going to fall in." He shuddered as he looked downstream to a spot where the water swirled around a huge boulder.

In the middle of the creek the water was almost to Jeff's waist. The current tore at his legs. Jeff moved inches at a time, his feet leaving the rocky bottom for only fractions of a second.

"We've got it made," Annie shouted as he edged past her.

Jeff moved his feet off a slick rock, braced himself against the current, and said, "Your turn." He hoped Annie wouldn't pull very hard.

"It's getting shallower," she called out.

He began to edge forward again. "Listen, Annie, next time you see a cop car, don't steal it—all right?"

They slogged through the knee-deep water on the far side of the stream. When they stepped up onto the bank, Annie sighed and slid out of her backpack. "I hope we don't have to do that again."

With their backs to each other, they changed their clothes. Jeff's hands shook so badly that he had trouble getting his pants buttoned.

"Are you all right?" Annie asked him.

"Compared to what?"

Annie smiled. "Let's walk and see if we can get warm that way. We only have one match, and I'd like to get as far as we can before we stop and make a fire."

Jeff bounced up and down while he rubbed his hands together. "Let's get moving then."

The wet clothes went into the bottom of the backpack. Jeff and Annie hurried along beside the new stream. Jeff studied the hill above them, looking for the road Darby had promised.

XV

Annie was dizzy. As long as she kept her head down and watched the ground in front of her feet, she could manage. But whenever she looked up quickly, the world began to spin.

She wondered if hunger was making her light-headed. People were supposed to be able to last a week or more without food, and she and Jeff were only on their second day.

She hoped Jeff wouldn't notice how unsteady she was, how she held on to trees whenever she got a chance. If he realized she was having problems, he'd insist on carrying the pack or stopping to rest.

She checked her watch and saw that forty-eight minutes had passed since they crossed the stream. She was determined to walk for a full hour before they stopped.

"Look up there!" Jeff shouted.

Annie jerked her head upward, and everything turned black. She grabbed a tree trunk to keep from falling. "What is it?"

"Just look right up there. See where it's kind of cut away? I'll bet that's the road."

Annie sank down onto the ground. "Let's rest for five minutes."

"I can't stand it, Annie. I'm going to climb up there and see, all right?"

Annie waved him on. She leaned back and watched him move up the hillside. She still couldn't see a cut.

"Here we go," Jeff yelled a moment later. "I knew it was the road."

Annie pulled herself to her feet. Now that they'd found the road, she could admit it to herself: She had thought they might die. For a day and a half she had kept that thought buried. Now she could look at it, sigh, and toss it aside. They were going to be all right.

When they started again, Jeff wanted to carry the backpack. Annie wondered if he could tell how dizzy she was. "We'll switch in a half hour," she said.

"I feel good," he told her. "When I saw this road, I felt like I'd just had a big steak."

"Don't talk about food."

He moved out ahead of her, looking for the easiest way around the fallen logs and the washouts that kept slowing them down. Even with the detours she figured they had traveled nearly a mile in thirty minutes. She wanted to keep going, but Jeff insisted upon taking the pack.

After that their pace slowed. Annie glanced at the late-afternoon sun and decided to wait only twenty minutes before she took back the pack. Behind her Jeff was singing again:

> Ants for you and ants for me.
> We'll have a red ant fricassee.

Annie kept her eyes fixed on the ground in front of her. She didn't see the body until Jeff yelled, "What is it?" and came trotting up beside her.

Fifty feet ahead of them Dave lay on the ground, his body bent backward. His eyes were closed, and his mouth hung open. "Is he dead?" Jeff whispered.

Annie dashed forward and dropped to her knees beside Dave. She put her hand on his cheek, which was so cold it startled her. "Dave!" she shouted. "Dave!"

"He's breathing," Jeff said. "I can see his chest move."

Annie began tearing at the wet knots. "Look in the pack. See if you can find a knife or something. She unbuckled the belt and pulled Dave away from the tree.

Jeff shoved the backpack aside. "Nothing here."

"Never mind. Go ahead and get a fire going." She reached into her shirt pocket for the last match. "Be careful with this."

"Don't worry," Jeff told her. "There are some matches in the pack."

"Thank heaven. He's freezing."

After a few minutes of yanking and pulling and getting nowhere, Annie settled down and tackled the knots like a math problem, taking one thing at a time. First she got the hands and legs separated. Then she untied Dave's wrists and rubbed the cold purple fingers for several minutes before freeing the legs.

By the time she had the legs untied, Jeff had the

fire blazing. "Let's get these wet clothes off him," she said.

Dave's eyes opened while they were taking off his shirt, but he didn't seem to notice anything. As she pulled off Dave's jeans, Annie sensed that Jeff was watching her. "Get those drawers off him," she said. "This is a pretty dumb time to be getting bashful."

All the clothes in the backpack were damp, so they eased Dave into Annie's sleeping bag and zipped it up. After moving him next to the fire, Annie began rubbing his hands again, opening and closing the fingers. "Go down and get some water, Jeff. We can feed him hot water anyway."

Jeff looked toward the creek. "You suppose Cracker's still around here?"

"He's probably sitting in the Alder Creek store right now," Annie said. "Go get that water."

While Jeff was gone, Annie spread Dave's sleeping bag and all the wet clothes beside the fire. When she ran out of room, she used a rock to drive sticks into the ground, then draped clothes over the sticks.

Afterward she began working Dave's fingers again. His eyes seemed to focus on her, and the fingers began to move without her help.

"Dave?" she said quietly. "Dave?"

He continued to open and close his hands.

"Are you hurt anywhere that doesn't show?"

For a minute the hands stopped moving. He seemed about to speak, then groaned and shook his head.

"All right. Listen to me." She watched Jeff make his way up the hill toward them. "Cracker pulled a gun on you and made you go with him. You got that? He pulled a gun on you and made you go. I don't ever want to hear different. You hear me? You know what I'm saying?"

Dave nodded, this time without stopping his hands.

"It looks like Mother Fletcher's laundry around here," Jeff shouted.

Annie heated water on the stove and managed to get Dave to drink several cups before he went to sleep. Jeff gathered more wood, then rummaged through Dave's pack. "What do you say to a fish dinner tonight?"

"Sounds great," she said.

"We've got a few salmon eggs and a couple of hooks left. I'll see what I can do."

For the rest of the afternoon Annie gathered wood and fussed with the drying clothes. When Jeff came plodding back up the hill, she knew from his face that he hadn't caught anything.

"I should have stayed here and helped you with the clothes," he said. "Maybe we could have made soup out of the salmon eggs."

Annie smiled. "Next time we go to a Laundromat, I'm going to get down and kiss the clothes dryer."

They sat in the middle of the steaming clothes and drank a cup of hot water, hoping it would quiet their stomachs.

"Tastes a little weird, doesn't it?" Jeff said.

"I don't know. I never drank hot water before."

Jeff grinned at her. "I can see why."

Annie glanced over at Dave, still rolled up in the sleeping bag. "While you were gone, he said Cracker made him come along. Put a gun on him and made him."

"Okay," Jeff said.

Annie looked at the water bubbling in the pot. "You want a second helping?"

Jeff was finishing his third cup of water when Dave turned to the side and opened his eyes. "How are you feeling?" Annie asked him.

Dave shook his head and sat up. "I'm doing better."

"You're plenty sore, I'll bet."

"I'll be all right."

"I hope you can walk," Jeff said. "We've got to get out of here in the morning. If I miss many more meals, I'm going to disappear."

Dave looked into the fire.

"You want some more hot water?" Annie asked him.

"I'll just take some cold water now," Dave said. He sipped water from a cup and studied the woodpile. "We'd better keep a good fire going. Maybe that'll keep the deer away."

"Deer?" Jeff said. "You're not scared of deer, are you?"

"Listen, last night they came right in here and licked my face and chewed on my shirt and stepped on me. I tried to yell and chase them off, but they kept coming back."

"Somebody must have been feeding them," Annie said.

"I can see the headline in the paper right now," Jeff shouted. "Boy Licked to Death by Deer."

"Dry up," Dave snapped.

"The attack of the wild tongues."

"Shut up, Jeff," Annie said.

"It's a great idea for a horror movie. First there was

The Shining and *The Haunting*. Now comes *The Licking*."

"I mean it," Annie shouted. "Shut up."

They sat and stared at the fire for a while. Jeff snickered now and then, but he didn't say any more.

"Who wants some more hot water?" Annie asked.

"Three's my limit," Jeff said. "Look, I've been thinking. Do we have anything sharp around here?"

"I think I still have my knife," Dave said. "It ought to be in the pocket of my jeans."

"Thanks, brother," Annie said. "I spent half an hour and tore back two fingernails getting you untied, and you had a knife in your pocket."

Dave smiled quickly. "I didn't remember it right then."

"We thought you were dead," Jeff said.

"I thought I was dead too." Dave's voice was just above a whisper.

Jeff found Dave's jeans and pulled the knife out of the pocket. "Here we go."

"What are you thinking about?" Annie asked him.

Jeff began digging through the woodpile. "I thought we could make a spear. What do you think? You think I've been drinking too much hot water?"

Annie shrugged. "Who knows?"

"If those deer came in close enough to lick Dave's face, we might be able to spear one."

Annie figured it was a waste of time, but she loved to hear the excitement in Jeff's voice. "It's worth a try, I guess." She pulled herself to her feet and helped Jeff look for a stick.

They found a sturdy pine limb about four feet long. Jeff trimmed off the side branches, then carved a notch in the end of the limb so that the knife handle would lie flat. Annie used Dave's shoelaces to tie the knife in place.

When the spear was finished, Jeff carried it over to where Dave was still lying in the sleeping bag. "Take a look at this beauty."

Dave ran his hand over the knots and handed the spear back to Jeff. "That's not much of a blade, but maybe it'll work."

"Just let that deer get close enough," Jeff said, "and I'll make it work."

While he helped Annie with the drying clothes, Jeff tried to quiz Dave about the deer—how many there were, which direction they came from. Dave didn't have many answers. "And I didn't get their names and addresses either," he said finally. "It was dark, and I was out of it most of the time."

Jeff tried to find a perch in one of the nearby trees but finally settled for the top of an old stump. "We'll let the fire burn down," he said. "You two just lie down and go to sleep. They won't come around until everything is quiet."

"If they don't show up pretty soon," Annie said, "you'd better get some sleep. We've got to get moving early."

They were quiet for a long time. Annie dozed for a time, then roused herself. "Jeff," she whispered, "you want to trade places for a while?"

"Are you kidding? How many times in my life do you think I'll get a chance for spear hunting?"

Annie smiled. "Okay, Tarzan. I just thought I'd offer."

"Dave," Jeff whispered, "when did Cracker go off?"

"Last night," Dave said after a minute.

"Did he remember the hundred he gave us for getting the first-aid kit?"

Dave suddenly laughed. "No. It must still be in the pocket of my blue shirt."

"That's good," Jeff said. "Now I can sit here and think about all the things I'm going to buy at the Alder Creek store."

"I don't think I can stay awake much longer," Dave said.

"That's fine," Jeff told him. "I'll wake you up when supper's ready."

Annie slept for a few minutes at a time, then jerked awake. Each time she looked around, she could see Jeff perched on the stump. He moved just often enough so that she knew he wasn't asleep.

When she first heard the rustling sounds, she thought Jeff had given up and decided to come to bed. She opened her eyes and saw him still huddled in the same spot. Then she heard the rustling again, on the far side of the fire.

Afraid to move, she listened as a backpack went clanging to the ground. An animal bounded away. For a minute or two everything was quiet, and Annie wondered if the deer were gone for good. Then she heard a pan scrape across the ground.

One of the deer seemed to be standing just behind her, but Annie didn't dare turn to look. The animal snorted and stamped its feet. Annie kept waiting for Jeff to move. Had he fallen asleep after all?

Then the animal stepped over her sleeping bag, putting one hoof on the corner. Annie stiffened but didn't move. She watched Jeff rise up on the stump, the spear held high. The deer snorted, turned its head back toward Annie, and took a step closer to the stump.

Then Jeff drove the spear home. The first thrust knocked the animal to its knees. Jeff sprang on top of it. The spear rose and fell again and again.

Annie scrambled out of her sleeping bag. The deer was on its side, kicking its feet wildly. Jeff was on top of it. "It won't die," he screamed.

Annie rushed forward. She remembered the times back on the farm when she had watched her father butcher animals. She snatched the spear with one hand and grabbed the animal's head with the other. She jerked the head back and used the knife to cut its throat. Then she stepped back and let the spear slip from her fingers. The deer kicked for a minute, then lay still.

Jeff staggered over and sank down on the stump.

"You did it!" Annie shouted. "You really did it."

Dave came toward them. "You got one. That's amazing."

Annie could hear a trace of anger in Dave's voice, but she didn't bother to analyze it. "I never thought you'd do it," she said to Jeff.

"It wasn't the way I thought it'd be," Jeff said quietly. He reached up and wiped his cheeks with his shirt sleeve. He stood up slowly and looked down at the deer. "Well, what are we waiting for?" he shouted. "It's suppertime."

XVI

Dave did the butchering, working slowly in the dim light of the fire. After helping him get the animal's carcass strung up to a tree limb, Annie and Jeff had drifted away. Now Annie was playing with the stove while Jeff poked at the fire. And Dave was left to do the dirty work.

"We'll start with the heart," he said. "Whenever old Lucky butchered an animal, we always had the heart and liver right away. He let the rest hang for a couple of days."

"Just give it to me, and I'll cook it," Annie said. "I don't want to talk about it."

She fried slices of heart in the small frying pan. When the first pan was cooked, she dumped the meat onto a metal plate and started another batch.

"No use being bashful," Jeff said, snatching a piece of the sizzling meat.

Dave wasn't sure he could swallow anything. He took a small bite of meat and chewed it slowly. "Ooh," he moaned. "Nothing ever tasted this good."

"Fantastic," Jeff said.

While the last slices of heart were cooking, Dave looked over at Annie. "You ready for some liver now?"

"I guess," Annie said.

"Wait a second," Jeff said. "Why's the rest of it supposed to wait?"

Dave shrugged. "I don't know. That's the way old Lucky always did it."

"Let's try some real meat," Jeff said. "An hour ago I would have given a hundred bucks for a piece of liver. Now I'm getting fussy."

Dave skinned the deer and cut thin slices from the front shoulder. Annie fried panful after panful until they all settled back and waved the plate away.

Jeff rubbed his stomach. "I thought I'd never get enough, but I think I made it—about three pans ago."

"I don't see what old Lucky waited for," Dave said. "That meat was good."

Annie set the pan aside. "I wonder if it's illegal to kill a deer that way."

"Probably," Jeff said, "but I'd rather be illegal than starving." He stood up and stretched. "We're out of water, and I've got to get cleaned up." He took their biggest pot and headed downhill into the dark.

"Be careful," Annie called after him.

Dave wrapped the deerskin around the entrails and dragged the whole bundle a short distance up the road. He came back and checked the deer carcass. It was tied to the limb, but the bottom barely cleared the ground. "I wish we could get it higher," he muttered.

"It'll be all right," Annie said. "It's only for a few hours anyway."

"You can't believe how cold this water is," Jeff shouted from below.

Annie and Dave crouched by the fire until Jeff came back. "Here you go," he shouted. "I only spilled about half of it." He spread out his blanket and lay down. "I'm just too beat for dishwashing."

"We'll just clean ourselves tonight," Annie said. "We'll save the dishes for morning."

Annie and Dave took turns pouring water on each other's hands until the water was gone. Still feeling sticky, Dave wiped his hands on his sleeping bag as he crawled in.

"I have a stomachache," Jeff called from his blanket. "And it hurts so good."

"Anybody got an Alka-Seltzer?" Annie asked.

Jeff laughed. "We've got plenty left for breakfast, but I'm not sure I'm going to want any breakfast."

"I want breakfast," Annie said. "I've had it with missing meals."

Dave lay a little way off from the other two. His shoulders still ached from being tied, and his ankles and wrists burned. He listened to Jeff chattering but didn't answer. It had happened again. Just as he always did, Jeff had done exactly the right thing. When they were close to starving, Jeff had killed a deer and saved them.

And Annie? She knew perfectly well that Dave had gone off and left them without any food, and right away she began covering for him. He wasn't even sure that Jeff knew what had really happened.

Dave knew he didn't deserve to be alive. By all rights he should have died out here. And it wouldn't

have been any loss. Annie and Jeff didn't need him.
He was as useless to them as he was to the rest of the
world.

But they had saved his life all the same, and what
had he done? He hadn't even bothered to say thank
you. He turned over in his sleeping bag. He could do
that much anyway. "Annie," he whispered. "Annie?"

"She's asleep," Jeff whispered back.

Dave lay there for a minute before saying, "Jeff?"

"Yeah?"

"That was good meat."

Dave awoke with a jerk. He looked up and saw the
blue-black of the early-morning sky. He moved his
arms slowly. His shoulders were stiff, biting with each
movement.

Then he heard the sound that had roused him out
of his sleep—a snorting, wheezing noise. He turned
his head and glanced toward the others.

The first thing he saw was the blackness of the
shape. A bear. He had never seen one up close, but
there was no mistaking it. The bear was pawing the
deer's carcass and tearing at it with its teeth. Beneath
its rear feet Annie lay huddled in her sleeping bag.

Dave reached an arm out of his bag and felt the
ground around him. His fingers closed on a stick—the
shaft of Jeff's spear.

The bear tore at the carcass and stepped back,
planting a back paw in the middle of Annie's bag.
Annie let out a scream.

Dave came out of his sleeping bag on the run. He
raised his stick as he dashed toward the bear. "Get
out!" He smacked the bear's rump with the stick,

putting all his strength behind it. The stick vibrated in his hand as if he had struck a rock.

The bear spun around. A huge paw batted the air. Dave stepped back and yelled, "Get out!"

For a moment the bear rocked back and forth, snarling. Dave hauled back the stick and smacked the animal on the nose. The bear jerked back and let out a noise that was somewhere between a growl and a whimper. It spun around, leaped over the low bushes, and went racing up the hill. Dave watched the animal disappear, then stood and listened to it crash through the brush.

"Oh, thank God," Annie moaned. "I don't know when I was ever so scared in my life." She sat up in her bag, then held her face in her hands.

Jeff climbed out of his blanket. "Wow," he said.

"Yeah." Dave sank down onto his sleeping bag. He could feel his pulse banging in his head and his chest.

For a minute all three of them just sat. Then Jeff stood up and walked to the fire. He stirred up the coals and began to pile on twigs and bits of bark. "I can't believe you," he said to Dave. "Who do you think you are, Davy Crockett? Taking on a bear with a stick—I can't believe it."

"I wasn't going to let that fat slob steal my breakfast," Dave said. He was surprised to hear his voice still trembling.

"You were great," Annie said. "I never saw anything like it in my whole life."

"This is going to make a great poem," Jeff said. " 'My brother, Dave, hunts bears with a stick.' Something and something 'and goes pretty quick.' Just give me a little time, and I'll work it out."

None of them went back to sleep. They crowded

around the fire and dozed a little, but sleep was finished for the night.

Dave lay back on the ground and smiled. He knew that the memories of this morning would stay with him the rest of his life. Like money in his pocket, these memories would be there to take out when he needed them.

On this morning he hadn't hung back and waited for somebody else. He had gone charging out after a bear. No matter how many stupid and wrong things he did, he would know that he didn't always act that way. Once he had done something special. He had gone after a bear with a stick.

"What day is it?" he asked.

"Who cares?" Jeff said.

"Let's see," Annie said after a minute. "It's Wednesday, I think." She mumbled and counted on her fingers. "No, it's Thursday morning."

"What day?"

Annie counted again before saying, "The twenty-first, I think. Yeah, that's right. The twenty-first."

Dave looked away, smiling again. The twenty-first of July. It was a date to remember. On the twenty-first of July Dave Bates had taken on a bear—and won.

XVII

Annie whistled while she turned the meat in the frying pan. And why not? Everything considered, they were in good shape. They had food, and they knew the way out. For a change things were going their way.

They had decided to take only cooked meat with them, so Dave was carving slices while she fried them and stuffed them into pots and plastic bags. She figured they should reach Alder Creek that day, but she kept cooking meat all the same. Judging by the past week, she knew better than to assume anything.

Jeff rolled up the sleeping bags while he worked on his new poem:

> All the bears hide in a cave
> And talk about the wild man Dave.
> He's not that big—just middle size.
> But watch it when he's got that look in his eyes.
> Legs of iron, arms of steel,
> Mean enough to make a grizzly squeal.

"That wasn't a grizzly," Dave said. "There aren't any grizzlies left in California. That's about the only thing I remember from my geography class."

"Don't mess with my poem," Jeff said. "Grizzly has the right sound. In fact, I think I'll call my poem 'Grizzly Dave.'"

"Anybody want another piece of meat?" Annie asked. "This last one won't fit into the sack."

"You talked me into it." Jeff snatched the meat from her. "You know," he said between bites, "this stuff isn't bad, but it's not half as good as it was last night."

"I can probably get a few more slices if you want them," Dave told Annie.

"I don't know what we'd put them in."

Dave looked at the carcass. "Between us and the bear we're not wasting much."

"Another verse," Jeff shouted.

> All the bears in their cave
> Tell about old Grizzly Dave.
> Eats a rabbit in a bite.
> Ate a deer in a single night.

"I don't get it," Dave said to Annie. "With all the practice he's had, how come his poems don't get any better?"

"Don't make fun of my poems," Jeff said. "I take applause, and I take money, but I don't take criticism."

Before putting on their packs, they went down to the creek for a cleanup. Jeff scrubbed the frying pan and set it aside. "If we weren't in such a hurry, I'd take a swim." He tossed a handful of water in Dave's direction.

"We can spare the time," Dave said, making a grab for him.

Jeff danced back out of the way.

> You may send bears running for their mother,
> But you don't scare your little brother.

"Let's go," Annie said. "We have an appointment in Alder Creek."

After a couple of hours they came to an area of deep canyons and steep sidehills where whole stretches of the road had been washed away by streams or wiped out by slides. At many of the washouts the three of them had to climb all the way down to the creek, pick their way along the bank, then scale a cliff on the far side.

Halfway up one of the steepest slides, Jeff began to laugh. Dave, who was dragging his pack over a rock, turned and glared. "What's so funny?"

"Look at this place," Jeff shouted. "Can you imagine trying to climb up here with your arm in a sling? It serves old Cracker right."

Dave began to smile. "And he took off at night. How far do you think he got on this road with a little-bitty flashlight?"

"Here's to you, Cracker," Jeff yelled. "I hope you had a wonderful trip."

Late in the morning Jeff came trotting back from scouting the trail. "I saw a guy down by the creek."

"Cracker?" Annie asked.

"No. This was a big, fat guy. As soon as he spotted me, he disappeared. What do you think?"

Dave looked around. "I think we keep right on going."

"Amen to that," Annie said.

"What do you suppose he's doing out here?" Jeff asked.

Dave started forward. "Growing pot probably. But it could be anything. And if he doesn't want to see us, we sure don't want to see him."

Annie followed along behind the others, her eyes sweeping the area above and below her. Once she thought she saw a movement in the brush, but she immediately looked away. When she glanced back a minute later, she couldn't see anything.

They didn't stop to rest for an hour.

In the early afternoon Annie led the way for a while, Jeff insisting upon taking her pack. She walked with a quick, easy step. It felt good to move her shoulders freely and to let her sweat-soaked shirt dry out.

As she reached the top of a rise, she let out a groan. The road ended a few feet in front of her. On the far hill, some fifty yards away, the road began again. In between was a sheer brown face.

"You might as well start cutting down the hill," she yelled over her shoulder. "There's a slide we'll have to go around."

Annie stood at the edge of the drop-off and tried to pick out a route for them to follow. Her eyes caught something unusual, and she stepped back. At the bottom of the far cliff was a mound of green—a man-made green, not something natural. She studied it carefully, waiting for it to move. When it didn't, she rushed back to Dave and Jeff.

"There's something at the bottom of the slide," she said.

"Dirt," Jeff said quickly.

Dave stopped and looked back at her. "What is it?"

"I can't tell. It's green, sort of like a tent or something."

Dave reached into his pocket for his knife. "Well, we'll have to check it out."

They were almost at the creek before they had a clear view of the slide. "Can you see it?" Annie asked. "It's just beyond those boulders."

Dave studied it for a minute. "I think it's a sleeping bag. But there can't be anybody in it. Nobody would sleep on the rocks there."

Annie thought of Cracker and shivered. "I hope not."

They moved forward slowly. Annie kept her eye on the bag, still afraid it might move.

The bag lay, half unrolled, at the bottom of the cliff. "Get the picture?" Dave asked with a grin.

"Sure," Jeff said. "Old Cracker got halfway up, dropped this thing, and didn't bother to come back after it." He picked up the bag and brushed it off. "This doesn't make me mad. I've about had it with that tinfoil blanket of mine."

While Jeff was cleaning off the bag and tying it to the pack, Annie took Dave aside. "You think Cracker's close by?"

Dave shook his head. "He's long gone."

Annie wished that he sounded more sure.

Twice that afternoon they saw people. The first was a fisherman, wading in the creek as he flicked his fly rod back and forth. Then there were two people stretched out in the sun on the far side of the creek. Annie was sure the highway couldn't be far.

Expecting to reach the road at any moment, they didn't make camp until sundown. They built an enormous fire, cut some willow sticks, and heated meat over the flames.

"It's sort of like a wienie roast," Jeff said.

Annie kept looking out at the darkness. Whenever she began to get sleepy, she remembered the bear standing over her and threw some more wood on the fire.

The night passed slowly. Once or twice she awoke and built up the fire. She thought she heard footsteps out beyond the firelight, but she never saw anything.

"Word gets around quick," Jeff said in the morning. "Once the word got out about Grizzly Dave, all the animals headed for cover."

Anxious to get moving, they tried eating the leftover meat cold. It was tough and stringy. Annie heated a few pieces, but nobody was very interested. They ate a little and stuffed the rest back into the plastic bag.

Annie tossed the bag into her pack. "I hope we don't need it."

"I figure to have my lunch at Alder Creek," Jeff said.

Dave lifted his pack. "Something happened to that meat. It tasted really good the first night."

Just beyond their camping place they came to a washout that took them most of an hour to get around. But then the road ran smoothly through a pine forest for a mile or two, and Annie began to think about Alder Creek again.

Two more washouts, both short and steep, took

another hour, and Annie wondered if they would be lunching on tough meat again. An open spot, which they were sure would be the county road, turned out to be an old homestead, where part of a rock chimney still stood.

In the middle of the clearing Jeff turned and looked back at the mountains. "It's hard to believe we came over those a few days ago."

Annie said, "Sure is," without turning around.

Leaving the homestead, they rushed along, scrambling over fallen trees, expecting to see the county road any minute.

Another steep washout forced them to backtrack and cut downhill to the creek. Jeff led the way through the rocks and debris at the bottom of the slide. "Every slide we come to, I figure it's the last one. But I keep being wrong."

"Stop right there!"

Annie turned and saw Cracker sitting in the shadow of the boulder they had just passed. He held the pistol leveled at Jeff's chest. "Don't do a thing," she whispered to Jeff.

"Tell Dave to get up here," Cracker said.

"I thought he was with you," Annie said.

"Don't give me that stuff, woman. I saw all three of you comin'." He raised the pistol until it was pointing at Jeff's head.

"Dave!" Annie called. "It's Cracker."

"You better get here in a hurry!" Cracker yelled.

"I'm here," Dave said, coming around the boulder.

Cracker turned the pistol toward Dave. "Just move over there by them, an' sit down." He looked at them and shook his head. "Y'-all are somethin'. Nothin' stops ya." He smiled, then broke into a giggle. "Except maybe me."

XVIII

Jeff was scared. There was something strange and wild about Cracker—quick, jerky movements, that weird giggle. Jeff cringed whenever the pistol waved in his direction.

"I can't believe our cruddy luck," Dave said, sinking down on the ground beside Annie.

"I'm glad to see y'-all," Cracker said. "I've had me a rough ol' time the last couple days."

"Good," Dave said. "You had it coming."

Cracker looked them over. "I guess y'-all don't have any food either."

Annie snorted. "How could we have any food? Some slimy lowlife stole it all."

"Yeah, we've got some," Dave said.

Cracker pointed the pistol at Jeff. "All right, kid, you get the food and bring it over here."

"Do what he says," Annie told Jeff.

Jeff stood up slowly and dug into Annie's pack for the bag of meat. He started toward Cracker, wondering how close he could get.

"Set it down right there." Cracker pointed to the ground in front of him. "Just play it nice an' cool. What is this stuff anyhow?"

"Deer meat," Jeff said.

Cracker opened the bag. "How'd you get a deer?" Jeff couldn't help smiling. "I speared it."

"Speared one. That's somethin'." He waved the pistol. "You move on back now, kid. I shot at a couple o' those dumb things, but they ran off. I was pretty sure I hit 'em, but it didn't do no good." He stuffed a slice of meat into his mouth. "Kinda chewy," he said after a minute. "But not so bad."

"You don't mind if I turn around, do you?" Annie put her back to Cracker. "The way you eat makes me sick."

Cracker's jaw tightened. His hand moved toward the pistol. Then he grinned. "Go right ahead, sister. Your face wasn't doin' a thing for my appetite."

After he had eaten several pieces of meat, Cracker wiped his fingers on his pants and pointed the pistol at Jeff. "If you speared a deer an' cut it up, you must have a knife. I'd better take it."

Dave reached into his pocket. "Come on. You think we're going after that pistol with a pocketknife?"

"Just toss it this way nice an' easy." Dave pitched the knife underhand. It landed at Cracker's feet. Cracker set down the pistol long enough to scoop up the knife and shove it into his pocket. Then, with the pistol in his hand, he picked up another slice of meat. "This stuff's all right. I'm tellin' ya, it's been tough. I 'bout froze to death last night. I lost my sleepin' bag awhile back, see."

"We found it," Jeff said when nobody else spoke.

Cracker giggled. "Well, you folks are just as handy as you can be, ain'tcha? I was needin' some help, I'll tell ya. Freezin'. Nothin' to eat. My ol' shoulder hurtin' like a fool. I figgered I was dyin'. If I hadn't had my little ol' bag o' coke, I just might have done it."

"Too bad you didn't," Annie said, still facing the other way.

"Serves you right," Dave said. "If you hadn't been so stupid, you'd be clear outa here by now. Tying me up. What was that supposed to prove?"

Cracker giggled. "That wasn't my best move. Just figgered wrong, that's all. It was a whole lot farther outa here than I thought." He reached for another slice of meat. "But it's all gonna work out. Just when I'm needin' help, here comes my old partner again."

Dave spit on the ground. "If you think I'm gonna help you, you're nuts."

Cracker swung the pistol over until the barrel was pointed at Dave's chest. "You'll help me, old buddy."

"I want to see this." Dave leaned back and laughed. "You only got one good hand to start with. You keep that gun pointed at me, and that leaves you with no hands. I just want to see you climb up that cliff over there with no hands."

"Don't even talk to him, Dave," Annie said. "He's nothing but slime."

"Turn around here, sister," Cracker called out. "I got a little job for ya. I want you to take the canteen down to the creek an' get me some water." He tossed the canteen toward her.

Annie didn't move. "Get your own water."

Cracker smiled. "Sister, you're gonna get me some water, an' you're gonna hurry your little self along, 'cause if you keep me waitin', I might start shootin' off your little brother's toes."

Jeff tightened as Cracker's pistol drifted toward him.

"I'll get the water." Annie snatched up the canteen and headed toward the creek.

"I just knew you were gonna change your mind," Cracker called after her.

Once Annie was gone, Cracker turned to Dave. "We got us some talkin' to do."

Dave looked away.

"No bull now. You know you're not gonna be my partner. I worked too hard for this stuff. But you can come out of this okay. How would you feel about a thousand bucks in your pocket?"

Dave shrugged.

"Look at the whole thing. If I promise you big money, you know I don't mean it. But a thousand bucks is different. It's easier to pay you than shoot you. You see what I mean?"

"Two thousand," Dave said quietly.

Cracker smiled. "Fifteen hundred. You get me outa here an' get me to San Francisco, an' it's yours." He reached for the meat again. "It's the best you can do, old buddy."

"You already owe us five hundred," Dave said. "All together that's two thousand."

Cracker giggled and bit into a piece of meat. "That's all, though," he said with his mouth full. "You get any more, an' you'll be worth robbin'."

Annie came tramping uphill, the canteen dangling on its strap from her right hand.

"Put it down easy before you get any ideas," Cracker told her.

Annie dropped the canteen in front of him. "Will there be anything else, sir?"

Cracker grinned. "Ornery, ain'tcha?"

Annie marched over and sat down beside Jeff, her back to Cracker.

"They got a deal going," Jeff whispered to her.

Annie sighed.

Cracker drank from the canteen and reached for the meat. "All right. I'm feelin' a little better now." He looked at Dave. "What about your family? What are we gonna do about them?"

Dave shrugged. "They won't hurt anything."

"Dave," Annie said, "don't get mixed up with that slime."

Cracker pointed the pistol at Annie's back. "She could get on a guy's nerves after a while."

"Be quiet, Annie," Jeff whispered.

"Don't pay any attention to her," Dave said. "She'll moan and fuss, but she won't do anything to get me in trouble."

"Maybe." Cracker sounded doubtful. "I can't see much advantage in havin' her around." He glanced at Jeff. "Or him either."

Jeff called out, "I won't make any trouble." The words sounded so silly that he wished he had kept quiet.

"Take it easy," Annie whispered.

"Might be just as smart to kill 'em," Cracker said. "Nobody'd ever know."

Jeff turned to Dave. The casual note in Cracker's voice scared him worse than any threat would have. He could imagine Cracker pumping bullets into them and then reaching for another slice of meat.

"Oh, sure," Annie shouted, turning to face Cracker. "What's a couple of murders?"

Cracker giggled. "That woke her up, didn't it?"

"Settle down, Annie," Dave said. "He's not gonna shoot you."

Cracker reached for another piece of meat. "Maybe."

"Come on," Annie said, her voice quiet. "You're not stupid enough to kill us. Why make that kind of trouble for yourself?"

Cracker pointed the pistol at her head. "I'll tell ya somethin', sister. Shootin' you wouldn't be all that tough." He lowered the pistol and hoisted himself to his feet. "All right, Dave. You can start earnin' your money. Pick up that canteen for me."

"Tell him to take a flying leap," Annie said.

Dave jumped up and walked forward. He scooped up the canteen, handed it to Cracker, then stepped back.

"That was smart, pard," Cracker said. "If you'd made one move toward me, I'd have blown you apart."

"Wise up," Dave said. "I just want to get outa here."

"Suits me." Cracker tipped up the canteen. He kept his eyes on Dave while he drank. "I'm doin' a whole lot better now." He tossed the canteen to the ground and looked at Annie. "But what about her?"

"She won't get in the way," Dave said.

Cracker shook his head. "I don't want her around. Or him either."

"Suits me," Annie said. "Jeff and I will stay right here."

Cracker smiled. "That's what I figgered." He looked at Dave. "Tie 'em up."

"Wait a minute!" Annie shouted. "You can't—"

Cracker stepped toward her, the pistol pointed at her face. "Sister," he said, "I can do any ol' thing I want. Now you just shut up, or I'll do things the quick way."

Annie turned to Dave, tears starting down her cheeks. "Dave, don't do this to us. Please."

"Settle down," Dave said. "I'll come back after you as soon as I can."

"Don't go with him," Annie pleaded. "He'll kill you when he's through with you."

Cracker giggled. "I don't think she trusts me."

"Take off your shoes," Dave told Jeff. "You too, Annie."

"Don't do this," Annie said. "We'll die out here." She turned to Cracker. "Let us go along. Please. I won't say a word. Not one."

Cracker shook his head. "If I didn't know better, I'd think that girl was beggin'."

"I am," Annie shouted. "I'm begging you. Please. Take us along."

Cracker turned away. "Hurry it up, Dave. We got things to do."

Dave didn't look at Jeff as he tied his ankles and his wrists. "Come back for us," Jeff whispered.

Dave turned toward Annie. "No." She began edging backward. "No!"

"Cut that out," Cracker yelled. He marched over and jammed the pistol barrel against Jeff's head. "You behave yourself, or I'll let the kid have it."

Annie sank down on the ground and began to sob. "Dave, why are you doing this?"

"Quit bawling," Dave said. "We're gonna come out of this whole thing with two thousand bucks."

"Oh, Dave, don't you ever learn anything?"

Once Dave began to tie Annie's ankles, Cracker stepped away from Jeff and picked up the canteen. "Make those knots good an' tight."

"Don't do this, Dave," Annie said quietly. "For once in your life use your head. That's slime money. We don't need it. We're not that kind."

Dave snorted.

"Don't be an idiot again."

"You're the idiot," Dave said. "You and your high-and-mighty ideas. If we're good little boys and girls and don't do anything naughty, then we won't be trash, and we can look down our noses at somebody. What a pile of crud! We *are* trash. Always have been. Who cares what we do? We're bottom of the barrel."

"You are," Jeff shouted. "That's for sure."

"And so are you," Dave shouted back. "The Bates family was always trash. That's why old Lucky has to go out and play the big man in his truck." He scooted away from Annie's feet. "Now put your hands together."

"You're so stupid," Annie said.

"I'll end up with two thousand bucks," Dave said. "That's not too stupid."

"And some dingaling will probably take it away from you," Jeff said. "I always figured you were adopted. You're too dumb to be related to us."

Dave tied a final knot and stepped away from Annie. "You two are making it real easy for me."

"Don't try to blame us," Annie shouted. "You're the one."

"Listen to me," Dave yelled. "I got one question

for you two hotshots. I'll be down there in San Francisco with two thousand bucks in my pocket. Why should I bother coming back here? Answer that one for me."

"Because we're your family," Annie said.

Dave snorted and turned away.

"Because you know—" Annie began.

Cracker pointed his pistol at her. "You're gettin' on my nerves, sister. Put a lid on it." He walked over and yanked at Annie's wrists. "Those knots are good an' tight, partner."

"What do you expect?" Dave said.

Cracker smiled. "You an' me are gonna get along fine." He looked at the backpacks. "You got any idea how far we are from that town?"

"Nope," Dave said.

"I'm tryin' to decide about the sleepin' bags. You think we'll get there today?"

"I thought we'd get there yesterday."

"I don't trust this country," Cracker said. "Let's take 'em."

Dave loaded his pack, taking the bag of meat, the frying pan, the stove, and two sleeping bags. He strapped the canteen around his waist and looked toward Cracker. "That's it."

"Let's move out then."

"Dave," Annie called out, "put the other sleeping bag around Jeff. Please. Do that much anyway."

Dave looked at Cracker.

Cracker shrugged. "I don't care. Just hurry up about it."

Dave unfolded the blanket and tucked it around Jeff. Then, without looking at Cracker, he threw the other sleeping bag over Annie.

"You're making a terrible mistake," she said.

Dave turned away from her. "Don't you ever shut up?"

Cracker walked over and tucked the bag around Annie's feet. "Wish us luck, sister. The better things go for us, the quicker ol' Dave will be back."

"Take Jeff with you," Annie said. "He can help out."

Cracker giggled. "You never give up, do ya?" He walked away from them, the pistol swinging back and forth.

"I wouldn't have gone anyway," Jeff told her. "I'm fussy about the company I keep."

Annie turned away from him, her body trembling. Jeff rolled onto his side and watched the two walk across the slide. At the bottom of the cliff Dave stopped and pointed out a path. Then he started up, scrambling from rock to rock. Cracker lagged far behind. From the awkward way Cracker was climbing, Jeff figured he still had the gun in his hand.

Annie sniffed a few times. "Are you all right?" she asked.

"More or less," Jeff said.

"Do you think you can get loose?"

Jeff tugged at the cords on his wrists, decided it was probably hopeless, and said, "I think so, but it'll take awhile."

"Same here," she said. "As soon as they're out of sight, we can start in."

"Annie," Jeff asked after a minute, "do you think Dave will come back for us?"

Annie was silent for a second too long before she said, "Sure he will. But we're not going to wait around."

Jeff shifted his weight and looked toward the cliff. Halfway up, Dave was standing in an open spot. Jeff wondered what was going on in Dave's mind. Could he just walk away?

Cracker was climbing slowly up the face of the cliff. Dave moved downhill and held out a hand, as if Cracker were one of the family. Jeff bit down hard.

Then Dave and Cracker were tumbling down the slope. "Dave jumped him!" Jeff yelled. "Dave jumped him!" The two rolled and struggled, then disappeared behind a rock. A moment later Dave stood up and held a fist high in the air.

"Attaway," Jeff yelled. He shouted and laughed while Dave dragged Cracker downhill. When he lost sight of them near the foot of the cliff, Jeff turned to Annie. "I knew he'd come through."

"Yeah." Annie's voice broke.

"Don't go crying now. It's all over." He watched her for a minute. "I don't know about you, but I figure I've been tied up long enough."

Cracker came into view, marching across the slide with his good hand on top of his head. Dave was ten feet behind him.

"Attaway, Grizzly Dave!" Jeff yelled.

Dave waved the pistol over his head.

When Cracker was a few steps away from Jeff, Dave shouted for him to stop. "Keep your hand on your head and lie down. I want my knife back."

Cracker dropped to his knees, then lay down. "No problem, pard."

Holding the pistol behind him, Dave reached down and took the knife out of Cracker's pocket. "Just don't move now."

"I wasn't fixin' to go nowhere," Cracker said.

Dave pulled the blanket off Jeff, then cut the strings on Jeff's wrists. "Here you go," he said, handing Jeff the knife.

"I knew you'd do it," Jeff said. "I knew it. I'm just glad you did it where I could watch. I enjoyed every minute of it."

Dave shrugged and stepped back. "Annie's waiting."

"No hurry," Annie said. Jeff cut the strings on his ankles, then rushed over and freed Annie. She stood up and rubbed her wrists. Tears fell from her cheeks onto her shirt.

"Cut it out," Jeff told her. "If you don't stop crying, you'll get me going too."

Annie walked over to Dave. "Thank you," she said. "And I'm sorry."

"You oughta be," Dave said. "I get tired of being treated like dirt. You're lucky I came back at all."

"I know," she said. "I'm sorry."

"Well, quit crying," Dave told her. "Everything's okay now."

"Hey, Dave," Jeff said, "I'll make up a poem for you later."

Dave grinned. "I can wait."

"Tell you what," Cracker called out. "I think we got some business to talk over."

XIX

"Old buddy, it looks like it's time to make us a new deal." Cracker smiled up at Dave.

"You know," Annie said, "I think we ought to tie something over his mouth. I'd like a little quiet right now."

Cracker laughed. "It doesn't matter whether I say it or not, sister. You know the score. You can't stand me, but you need me. Right?"

"We don't need you at all," Annie said.

Dave looked at Annie, then found himself looking at the pack wrapped around Cracker's waist. One hundred thousand dollars' worth of cocaine. The old dreams began to stir. He saw himself heading that new pickup toward the drive-through window.

"Even shares, Dave," Cracker said. "I've got the contacts, an' you've got the pistol. Let's get on out of here an' cash it in. In a couple days I can head south, and you can head anywhere you feel like. We gotta work together." He turned and smiled at Annie. "No hard feelin's, sister."

"Drop dead," Annie told him.

Cracker laughed.

"You know what we ought to do," Jeff said. "We ought to tie him up and leave him here. Give him a little of his own medicine."

Annie turned to Dave. "Keep your pistol on him. I want to go through his pockets. There's five hundred dollars somewhere."

Cracker lay back on the ground and put his hand on his head again. "I'm not about to cause any trouble. The money's inside my shirt pocket."

"I'll get it," Jeff said. He unbuttoned the pocket and drew out a roll of bills. "I hope this stuff isn't counterfeit."

"It's real," Cracker said.

Jeff moved back and began counting the bills. "You know whose picture is on the hundred-dollar bill?"

Dave laughed. "I don't even care."

"This is great," Jeff said. "There's five hundred and fifty here. That gives us a little interest."

"Put the fifty back in his pocket," Annie said.

Jeff looked over at her. "What?"

"You're kidding," Dave said.

"We made a deal," Annie said. "We told him we'd help him get to Alder Creek for five hundred dollars."

"What about him?" Jeff began. "He's been—"

"We're different from him. We made a deal, and we're going to stick to it."

Dave shook his head. "Annie, you're crazy."

"It runs in the family," she said. She looked down at Cracker. "We'll help you as far as the county road. Then you're on your own." She took a bill from Jeff's pile and stuffed it into Cracker's shirt pocket.

Cracker grinned at her. "Lady, it's a pleasure doing business with you."

"Shut up," Annie said. "We'll take you that far, but we don't need any of your talk at all."

"You're callin' the shots, sister." Cracker sat up. "I guess we might as well get started."

"Not so fast," Annie said. "Nobody told you to sit up."

"What is this?" Cracker said.

Annie stepped back. "I want you lying flat out. You can either do it yourself, or we can do it for you."

Cracker lay back on the ground. "I'm easy to get along with."

Annie came over and put one foot on Cracker's wrist. "Dave, if he even moves, let him have it."

"I couldn't move if I wanted to," Cracker said.

"Okay, Jeff," Annie called, "unbuckle his pack."

"Now just a minute," Cracker said. "There's no—" He stopped when Annie shifted her other foot onto his arm.

Jeff unbuckled the daypack and yanked it free. "Here you go, Annie."

Cracker sat up as soon as Annie stepped back. "Be real careful there. That stuff's expensive."

Annie unzipped the pack and removed the plastic bag. "The way I figure it," she said, "this wasn't part of the deal."

"That stuff's gonna turn your life around, sister," Cracker said. "Anything you want—it's all yours. Right there's your chance to change everything—to go for the big one."

Annie held up the bag and stared at it for a minute. "You know what I think? I think we don't need this stuff."

"If you don't want it," Cracker called out, "that's up to you. I'll take it off your hands." He let out a giggle. "But you can probably figger out somethin' to do with all that money."

Dave watched Annie untie the outer bag and slip the rubber band off the inner one. He tried to figure how many pickups that one package would buy. None of it seemed real.

Annie looked at Jeff, then at Dave. "Who needs this stuff? All it does is mess up people's brains." She pointed at Cracker. "Look at him. A giggling moron. Who needs it?"

"Careful, sister," Cracker said with a smile. "You're gonna hurt my feelin's."

"I figure we've got enough trouble without this stuff." Annie reached into the bag.

"Be careful!" Cracker yelled. "Don't spill it whatever you do!"

Annie brought out a handful of white powder and threw it out across the rocks. Some of the powder drifted with the wind. She took a few steps, dug into the sack, and brought out another handful.

Cracker leaped to his feet. "What are you doin'? You're nuts!" He ran toward Annie.

Dave stepped in front of Cracker, aiming the pistol at his chest. "Hold it!"

"Stop!" Cracker yelled, dodging around Dave.

Dave stuck out his foot. Cracker tripped and went sprawling to the ground. He screamed when his wounded shoulder smacked down, but he scrambled to his knees.

"Here!" Dave yelled, handing the pistol to Jeff. He piled onto Cracker, slamming him down again.

Cracker tried to shake loose, but Dave grabbed his neck and pushed his face into the dirt.

Cracker yanked and squirmed. "Dave," he yelled, "don't let her do it." That's your life she's throwin' away."

"This is fun," Annie called. She scattered another handful.

"So's this," Dave yelled, shoving Cracker down again.

Cracker suddenly quit struggling. "Stop her, Dave. Stop her while there's some left. She's crazy."

Dave glanced over at Annie and started to laugh. "Jeff," he said, "you think Annie's crazy?"

Jeff grinned. "I think it runs in the family."

XX

"Save me a little," Cracker yelled, squirming away from Dave. "Just a little bit anyway." He jerked free and got to his knees.

"Look out!" Jeff yelled, pointing the pistol at Cracker.

Dave let out a roar. He leaped onto Cracker's back and rode him to the ground again.

Cracker screamed and kicked, then went limp. "Make her stop, Dave."

Dave looked up at Jeff. "What's the date?"

"July twenty-second," Jeff said. "You went after the bear on the twenty-first, and that was yesterday morning."

"Hey, Annie," Dave yelled, "remember that date. July twenty-second. That's the day you threw away a hundred thousand bucks." He leaned back and laughed, his whole body shaking.

"It was worth it," Annie said. "That was fun."

When Annie turned the bag inside out, Dave slid

off Cracker's back and stood up. Jeff handed him the pistol.

"I can't believe it," Cracker said, getting up slowly. "I can't believe anybody in the world could be so dumb." He wandered away from them. Jeff watched him run his finger along some rocks and then bring it to his mouth.

"Well," Annie said, "let's hit the road. I don't know about you two, but I wouldn't mind something for dinner besides deer meat."

"I wish I had a movie of that," Dave said. He pulled on his pack while Jeff helped Annie into hers.

"Jeff, you think that was dumb?" she asked.

Jeff shook his head. "Nah, cocaine's not our style. The Bates gang swipes TV sets and cop cars. We're not dopers."

Annie laughed and gave him a shove. "Get out of here."

"Let's go," Dave said, sticking the pistol in his belt.

Cracker was still moving around the rocks, his eyes on the ground.

"You coming?" Annie asked him.

"What difference does it make?"

"You paid for a trip all the way. You might as well come along."

"I just can't believe you did that."

"You know what they say," Annie said. "No use crying over spilled coke."

"If he wants to stay here and suck on the rocks, let him," Dave called. "We're leaving."

"Come on, Cracker," Annie said. "You might as well come along."

Cracker looked around and shook his head. "I can't

believe it. I got shot, almost starved to death. And for what?"

"Maybe you learned something," Annie said, laughing easily.

Cracker glared at her. "I shoulda shot you the first night."

For the rest of the morning they made their way across and around a series of washouts. At midday they stopped by the creek and chewed on cold deer meat. "This stuff gets worse and worse," Jeff said.

Keeping the pistol beside him, Dave sat apart from the others. When they were ready to leave, Annie went over and spoke to him. Then she took the pistol and removed the bullets. She threw them, one by one, across the stream and into the brush beyond.

"We don't need a gun," she told Jeff. "We just need to make sure Cracker doesn't have one."

Cracker stared into the swirling waters of the creek. "Unbelievable," he muttered.

An hour later the road they were following ran into a hiking trail. The entrance to the road was blocked off by a row of rocks, and an arrow warned hikers to stay on the trail.

"You have the feeling we made a bad choice?" Jeff said.

Annie stood and looked down the trail. "It must cross the creek right down there. I guess there wasn't any trail when Darby used to come through here." She shook her head. "I wonder how much time we could have saved if we'd known."

"That's all right," Jeff said. "We don't like to do things the easy way anyhow."

They followed the smooth trail for a mile before

reaching the unpaved county road. Half a dozen dusty cars were parked beside the trailhead. "This is it!" Jeff yelled, jumping up and down in the road. "We made it!"

"It's about time," Dave said.

Jeff examined the wooden sign and called out, "Alder Creek, two—that way." He pointed to his right. "Kirkland, nine—that way." He spun around and pointed in the other direction. "Tough choice, huh?"

"Y'-all goin' to Alder Creek?" Cracker asked Annie.

"You bet."

"Then I'm goin' the other way."

"Suits us just fine." She turned to Dave. "Give him the pistol. We don't need it."

Dave shrugged and handed Cracker the gun, handle first. As Cracker took it, he kept staring at Annie. Jeff was afraid Cracker might throw the gun at her.

Annie slipped off her backpack and brought out the first-aid kit. "There isn't much here, but you might as well take it."

Still staring at her, Cracker shoved the pistol into his belt and reached for the kit.

"And here's your flashlight," Annie said.

Cracker stuffed them into his pack, jerked the zipper closed, and walked away.

After helping Annie slip on her pack, Jeff glanced toward Cracker, who was standing in the road with his back to them. "Bye-bye, Cracker," he said. "You ever feel like going camping again, don't call me."

Cracker spun around, his pistol in his hand. "You didn't know I had bullets in my pocket, did you?" He kept the gun trained on Jeff's middle. "You got another joke for me?"

"Don't," Jeff called out. "Please."

Then the pistol moved past him and stopped on Annie. "You're the one I've been waitin' for." Cracker walked toward them, his eyes fixed on Annie.

"Come on, Cracker," Dave said. "It's all finished."

Cracker smiled and kept walking toward them. "No way, buddy. You think I'm just gonna walk away? After what she did to me?"

"Don't do it," Dave shouted. "It's a sucker move. You shoot a girl, you're finished. That's the gas chamber."

Cracker laughed. "Who cares? This is worth it."

"Don't, Cracker," Jeff yelled. "Please."

Annie let out a moaning noise.

"You're too smart for this," Dave said. "You've had rotten luck, but you're too smart to throw it all away."

Cracker stopped ten feet away. The pistol was still pointing at Annie's chest. "This is gonna be pure pleasure," he said. "You earned this."

"Wait!" Dave screamed. "Don't do it! Don't shoot her!"

"No!" Jeff yelled.

Annie screamed as Cracker's finger squeezed the trigger. The pistol made a dull click.

"Don't I wish," Cracker said disgustedly. He shoved the pistol into his belt, turned his back, and marched away.

For a minute the three of them stood and watched him go. Then Dave yelled, "I'll kill him." He ran to the side of the road and grabbed up a rock.

"Let him go," Annie said.

Dave glanced at her, then heaved the rock. It

sailed past Cracker's head. Cracker kept walking straight ahead at the same pace.

"Let him go," Annie said again. "It's over."

Dave picked up another rock but let it fall. "Yeah."

When Cracker disappeared around a bend in the road, Jeff said, "Bye-bye, Cracker."

Annie straightened her pack and let out a long breath. "Nobody has to know we ran into him. We just came over the mountains. There's nothing at all to tie us to him."

"Except the money," Dave said. "You're not planning to throw that away, are you?"

Annie laughed. "I've done enough throwing away for one day."

They saved out one fifty-dollar bill and tucked the rest of the money into their shoes and sleeping bags. Then they started down the dusty road toward Alder Creek.

Two pickups passed them while they walked, both heading in the wrong direction. "Don't pick up any hitchhikers," Jeff yelled at them.

When they spotted the first houses, Dave stopped in the road. "What do you think? Should one of us go in, or should we all go together?"

"Let's go together," Annie said. "If there's a sheriff waiting for us, it'll save us from having to decide what to do next."

"This is tough," Jeff said when he spotted the gas pumps in front of the store. "I have to decide between an Eskimo pie and an ice-cream sandwich."

"Have both," Dave told him.

"I plan to. But I have to decide which one to have first." He looked over at Annie. "You think fifty bucks will be enough? I figure I can eat that much by my-self."

"We're really here," Annie said. "We made it."

"You'd better not start crying," Dave said.

They were almost to the store when Jeff saw it. A red Peterbilt rig was parked on the far side. "It's Daddy," he shouted, and raced toward the truck. "He got the letter."

Lucky Bates leaped down out of the cab and grabbed up Jeff. He held him tightly while he reached out for the others. "I'm so glad to see you," he said. "I've been sitting here for three days, waiting. I didn't know where else to go. Thank God you're safe."

Dave stepped back. "That's enough bawling and hugging," he said. "We're starving to death."

Lucky carried his ice chest up onto the porch of the store. While the three of them drank root beer, he sliced tomatoes and cheese for ham sandwiches.

Dave and Annie eased over close to Jeff. "Listen," Dave said, "don't tell Lucky about the money."

Jeff nodded. "Don't worry."

"This year we're going to have some decent school clothes," Annie said.

"Come and get 'em," Lucky shouted. "You don't want to let these beauties get stale."

While they ate, Jeff fed the rest of the deer meat to an old dog that came begging. "Hey, Dad," he asked, "when you kill an animal, how come you hang it for a while before you cut it up?"

"Meat's terrible if you don't," Lucky said. "Might as well chew shoe leather."

Jeff grinned. "That's what I figured."

When they couldn't hold any more, they piled into
the cab of the Peterbilt. "We're heading back to
Cooperville," Lucky told them. "I talked to the depu-
ties over there and explained about Grace running
off and all. They'll give you a good talking-to, but it'll
be all right."

"Are you sure?" Annie asked.

"You bet, darling. You'll be put on probation, but
things will be okay." Lucky leaned back in the seat.
"Yes, sir, it's all gonna work out. I figure I've learned
my lesson. I thought I'd lost you kids, and I couldn't
have lived with that."

"It wouldn't have made us too happy either," Jeff
said.

"I'm going to do things different from now on,"
Lucky declared. "I figure it's a whole new ball game
from here on."

Jeff wondered how many times he had heard
Lucky Bates say those same words. He glanced at
Dave and Annie, and they both nodded and grinned.

They knew better.

Lucky Bates wasn't going to change. Sooner or
later Jeff and Annie and Dave would be on their own
again.

But Jeff wasn't worried. The three of them could
handle anything that came along.

Exciting, action-packed adventures by

P. J. PETERSEN

THE BOLL WEEVIL EXPRESS $2.95 91040-4

Three teenagers run away from home, only to find that the struggle to survive is harder than they thought.

CORKY AND THE BROTHERS COOL $2.75 91624-0

Tim has a great time with Corky, the new guy in town, until their pranks get them into some deep troble.

GOING FOR THE BIG ONE $2.95 93158-4

Left on their own, three teenagers camp in the mountains in search of their father.

HERE'S TO THE SOPHOMORES $2.50 93394-3

It's sophomore year, and Michael is ready for some fast action—then his best friend becomes the best known and most controversial guy in school.

NOBODY ELSE CAN WALK IT FOR YOU $2.95 96733-3

A backpacking trip turns into a nightmare when the hikers are terrorized by a group of motorcyclists.

WOULD YOU SETTLE FOR IMPROBABLE? $2.95 99733-X

When Arnold, teen con artist and delinquent, joins Michael's ninth grade class, both Arnold and his new classmates have trouble adjusting to each other.
